CARNIVAL IN PARIS

Books by

Natalie Savage Carlson

For Freddy Scheibl

CARNIVAL

pictures by Fermin Rocker

HARPER & ROW, PUBLISHERS, NEW YORK AND EVANSTON

Natalie Savage Carlson

IN PARIS

CARNIVAL IN PARIS

CONTENTS

CHAPTER ONE

Uncle Simon's Farm

Once there was a little French girl named Nelly Flandin who lived two different lives. Sometimes she felt like two little girls put together.

During the school year she and her brother Marc lived with Uncle Simon and Aunt Barbe in a quiet farm village west of the great city of Paris. It was such a quiet village that it might have been a hundred miles from Paris. In its shoulder-to-shoulder buildings lived farmers and their families and their beasts and fowls.

It was so quiet that the crowing of the roosters in the morning was enough to wake the whole village without the use of clocks. It was quiet and deserted during the day when the grownups were working out in the fields and the children in school. It was even more quiet at night when all the inhabitants were in bed and all the doors and gates bolted.

Nelly had to walk to the end of the main street to the girls' school. She and Marc walked there together because the boys' school was right beside it. They carried their books and papers in big brief cases like all the other village children. And like the others they wore aprons to keep their clothes clean. Nelly's was checked blue and white and Marc's a solid gray.

But their schoolmates knew that they were different. It

wasn't only Nelly's little golden earrings or Marc's acrobatics. They were like the wild birds that fly into the hen yard and stay among the farm fowl only long enough to feed upon the grain and scraps.

Nelly and Marc were the children of carnival workers. During their carefree summer vacations, they lived like Gypsies in the red caravans of the Petit Cirque Flandin. They traveled all over France with their circus, following the carnivals and the fairs. They lived with Papa and Mama, their older sister Odile, and their big brother Fernand. Of course, there was Uncle Bruno too.

And they lived again among animals who could do such remarkable things—animals so much smarter than the big horses who pulled Uncle Simon's carts, the fowls that pecked between the cobbles, and the black and white Breton cow in the pasture behind their courtyard.

"You are lucky as a blue flower," said a schoolmate to Nelly enviously. "I wish my parents were carnival people. I wish they traveled all over the country."

"Oh, no, you don't," cried Nelly. "You have a whole family, but ours is cut in two most of the time."

It seemed so long ago that Nelly and Marc had seen their own family. It had been in October when Aunt Barbe had come for them on the bus. Nelly and Mama had cried and clung to each other, but Papa had tried to joke.

"Go back to the village and work up such a clever act that we won't be able to get along without you," he had said, his eyes looking watery.

But Uncle Bruno was not one to joke. "You don't know when you're well off," he told them. "Carnival life is hard work, what with trying to keep ahead of the bill collectors and finding enough food for animals and humans at the same time."

Queer old Uncle Bruno. He really looked more like a farmer than a carnival worker, even when he wore the long-tailed coat that didn't fit him right. Papa, too, and Mama in her torn sweater and slacks. But when Odile was dressed in her velvet shorts and silk blouse, she looked as if she belonged in the world of loud music and bright lights. And Fernand with his nose painted red and his hair combed forward, doing funny things to make the audience laugh, could never have lived in a quiet farm village lost in fields of leeks and cabbages.

And just imagine the gray ponies, Grisette and Guy, pulling carts or plows.

Or the trained dogs, Dodo, Bobo, and Coco, doing nothing but lying around in the courtyard or following the tilt carts into the fields.

Or the saucy goats, brown Noisette and white Nanette, staidly eating hay so they could make milk.

4

Nelly was thinking of all of them as the March school day ended. She quickly shoved a few books and her pencil box into her brief case. She squeezed in line to march out the door. The teacher always stood there with a long loaf of bread in her hand. As the girls filed by and politely wished her good-by for that day, she tore off a piece of bread for each one.

Munching the bread made the walk back through the village seem much shorter. Marc joined her and soon they outdistanced the other pupils.

"I'm so happy," declared Nelly. "Spring is here and the family must be in Poitou by now. It won't be long until summer, and tomorrow is Thursday so it's a holiday."

"School won't be out until July," Marc reminded her. "And after tomorrow's over it will be school again. Whoever divided up school time and vacation didn't do it fairly."

"But the Easter holidays are coming," insisted Nelly. "Then it will be so much closer to the time we join the family."

"It will be half a geography and a pile of spelling tablets before we go," said Marc glumly. "Besides, I can't do more than ten somersaults, one after the other. I want to be able to do fifty—around and around in a circle. Perhaps Papa will want me to stay with the circus full time then."

They both remembered what Papa had said about working up such a clever act that the circus wouldn't be able to do without them. Nelly looked glummer than Marc. She had almost broken her arm trying to hang from the clothesline by her knees. And she had surely broken the line. Uncle Simon wouldn't let her perform on the big Percheron horses. And Aunt Barbe didn't approve of carnival life.

Nelly swallowed her last bite of bread and skipped ahead of Marc. They hurried along the village street, which was deserted except for a very old woman who sat in front of her door, knitting away the quiet hours into a gray sock.

"I must get supper started before Aunt Barbe gets back from the fields," said Nelly, quickening her steps.

"And Uncle Simon told me to drive the cow home and milk her," remembered Marc. "Stupid old cow! She doesn't know how to do anything but eat grass and moo. She's ignorant."

Nelly agreed with him. "All the animals and fowl here are ignorant," she said. "All but Arabelle. She's smart."

"Pooh!" scoffed Marc. "She's only a goose. She's so stupid she follows you around and thinks you're her mother or something."

They passed the door of their house and headed for the arched gateway that led to the courtyard. It was surrounded by outbuildings covered with the same sway-back and faded red tiled roof that sheltered the house. Chickens and ducks were running loose among the cobbles. Across in the shed a broken wagon stuck its tongue out saucily at the barn.

The fowl seemed mildly interested in the children's ar-

rival, and the ducks broke into chatty quacks as if to tell the gossip of the day.

"Here comes Arabelle now," cried Nelly.

Arabelle always came to meet her. She had started that when she was a downy gosling and a neighbor had given her to Nelly so she wouldn't miss the circus animals so much.

Nelly patted Arabelle's white feathers. "She is not stupid," she maintained. "I'll prove to you that a goose can be smart if somebody takes the trouble to teach her something."

"And what will you teach her?" asked Marc mockingly. "How to read and write and work arithmetic problems?"

His words gave Nelly a wonderful idea.

"I'll teach her some clever circus tricks," she decided. "I don't want to be an acrobat anyway. I get scared when I'm way up high. I'll teach Arabelle to walk a tightrope and ride on a pony's back and then I won't have to."

"Honk, honk," said Arabelle with enthusiasm.

"How can you teach her to ride on a pony's back?" asked Marc. "We won't see the ponies until next summer."

"I'll teach her on old Forte," said Nelly. "He's gentle."

Marc smirked. "If you can get Arabelle to stand on Forte's back when he is walking," he said, "I'll stand on his back too—on my head."

Nelly's brown eyes sparkled. "Oh, wouldn't that be a wonderful act?" she gasped. "You standing on your head on ponyback with Arabelle on your feet."

"I'm not going to share my act with any goose," said Marc. "How would I know if the audience was clapping for me or for a silly goose?"

When Nelly had an idea, she had to begin work on it right away. She and Marc quickly tossed their brief cases into the house, then they made for the stable, with Arabelle following at a waddle. They sniffed the familiar smell of hay and leather and beasts. If they closed their eyes, they could imagine themselves in the great red truck of the Petit Cirque Flandin.

Old Forte tried to look around his fat hindquarters to see who was coming in. He heaved a great sigh of relief to see that it was no one with a bridle. He went back to munching his hay.

Nelly scrambled up into the manger. She stroked Forte's thick mane. "Poor old Forte," she said sympathetically. "You can't help it if you don't know how to walk on your hind legs or sit down on a stool. Nobody ever taught you."

Marc helped her lift Arabelle onto the horse's back. The goose stood there for a few moments trying to get used to such a strange perch. She cocked her head at the horse's ears. Forte turned his own head toward her. Then he contemptuously shook his skin as if he were being bothered by a fly. Arabelle gave a nervous hiss. This bothered Forte's ears. He turned them back, switched his short tail, then lazily kicked his lame leg.

Arabelle hissed louder. She went flying over his tail and fled out the doorway.

"Ho, ho, ho," laughed Marc, turning a somersault into the hay. "Arabelle, the flying goose." He picked himself up, brushed off the hay, bowed, and pretended that he was

Uncle Bruno announcing the next act in the Petit Cirque. "Arabelle, the learned goose, will now fly off the stage," he shouted. He was so amused by his own words that he continued them. "She will fly over the audience with Nelly, the goose girl, on her back."

Nelly was filled with rage. She didn't know whether to be mad at Marc or Arabelle or Forte. But it was easiest to take her temper out on the horse. She kicked his broad chest. "Why did you have to frighten Arabelle?" she demanded.

Then she grabbed a handful of straw and ran to throw it on Marc. He ducked and scooted out the door. Nelly chased him with the straw, but he was so fast she couldn't catch up with him. To show off his speed, he took time to turn a couple of somersaults on the way. He started for the archway, with Nelly following him into the street. They both raced past the woman who was too old to do anything but sit and knit.

Nelly angrily threw the straw at her brother, but the wind carried it back into her own face. The chaff blinded her eyes and the straw clung to her long brown hair.

When she was able to open her eyes, she saw a procession of farm carts coming down the road from the fields. Uncle Simon's was in the lead. He was riding on the horse, and Aunt Barbe was hunched among her petticoats in the cart, a faded blue scarf covering her head.

Nelly remembered with a start that she and Marc had forgotten all about their farm chores.

CHAPTER TWO

The Unexpected Visitor

Marc raced to meet the cart coming home from the fields. Nelly followed on his heels. Arabelle came behind, waddling from side to side in her haste, and honking, "Wait for me. Wait for me."

Uncle Simon stopped the horse and climbed down. He was as whiskery as a barley head and wore the patched blue overalls which Aunt Barbe was always trying to give to the scarecrow.

He hoisted the two children onto the horse's back and walked beside them. At sight of this Arabelle turned on her webbed toes and ran back to the courtyard, honking wildly. She made it quite clear that she could never be taught to have anything to do with horse or pony.

Aunt Barbe loosened the scarf under her chin. "Are the potatoes boiling yet?" she asked Nelly. "And did you put the soup back on the stove to heat?"

Nelly's head lowered over the horse's mane. She screwed her fingers around the high wooden point of the collar. "I forgot," she confessed. "I didn't think about it until I saw the carts coming back."

"She was too busy trying to train a goose to ride horse-

back," laughed Marc behind her. Then his own head lowered. He hadn't driven the cow home from the pasture and milked her. "And I forgot the stupid cow," he added soberly.

"Do you think she is stupid when you drink her milk?" asked Uncle Simon.

"If she tried to dance on her hind legs like a circus beast and forgot to make milk, she would be stupid," added Aunt Barbe.

Nelly uneasily curled a wisp of the horse's mane around her finger. "I don't think Arabelle is stupid," she said. "I'm going to teach her to do some wonderful tricks."

"There is time for a goose to do tricks and another time for her to lay eggs," said Aunt Barbe as they drove into the courtyard. "And there is a time for my little niece to play with her pet, but it is not when she should be doing her chores."

In his own shame, Marc hurried down the hill behind the courtyard to fetch the cow home for the evening milking. In his place, Nelly helped Uncle Simon unhitch the horse from the cart. Then she went to the kitchen, where her aunt was peeling potatoes.

Silently Nelly began to set the table. She laid the cutlery on the checked oilcloth. She set the glass of pale anemones in the exact center.

"Perhaps you better put some more salt in the soup while I see what's keeping our men," said Aunt Barbe.

Nelly scarcely heard her words. Her mind was far away. She was another Nelly, a famous animal tamer in a cage full of fierce lions and tigers. They snarled and clawed the air, but they obeyed her every command because she was fearless Nelly Flandin, who had started her remarkable career by teaching a goose to perform.

"Nelly," cried Aunt Barbe in such a stern voice that it set all the lions and tigers fleeing into thin air, "you are putting sugar in the soup!"

In startled shame Nelly looked at her hand. It was holding the sugar bowl instead of a long snaky whip—or the salt box.

Marc came into the room followed by Uncle Simon, who was carrying a half-filled pail of milk. His uncle set the milk down and Aunt Barbe peered into the pail.

"Is that all the milk that lazy creature gave us?" she asked, forgetting that she had defended the cow before.

"Marc spilled it," explained Uncle Simon. "He was trying to balance the pail on his head."

The boy stood sullenly with downcast eyes while Aunt Barbe gave him his second scolding.

But everyone was in a good mood by the time supper was on the table. No one can drink hot homemade soup and be completely unhappy at the same time.

"And the sweet taste is pleasing," said Aunt Barbe to Nelly. "Perhaps you have invented a new kind of soup."

The pleasant supper was interrupted by a heavy, impatient thumping on the door. It was loud enough to send everyone in the village running to answer his own door.

Uncle Simon was outraged. "Such a racket at this hour," he declared.

"Perhaps there is a fire or someone is dying," cried Aunt Barbe.

She reached the door first and swung it open. On the threshold stood Fernand, the clown of the Petit Cirque Flandin, who should have been down in Poitou. And he didn't look full of fun. His eyes were worried, the corners of his mouth drooped, and his clothes hung as loosely as if they were fastened to his shoulders with clothespins.

"Is somebody dead?" cried Aunt Barbe.

"Only a monkey we bought in Marseilles," answered Fernand. "It caught pneumonia. Everyone else is well and they all send their love."

Nelly ran to him and threw her arms around his waist. Excited as she was, she noticed how thin he felt inside his loose clothing.

"Come to the table and have some food," insisted Aunt Barbe. "Then you can tell us all about it. Never tell bad news on an empty stomach." She was sure from his appearance that he must be bringing news of some misfortune.

Nelly and Marc could hardly wait for their brother to finish his soup. He gulped it down as fast as he could, like a starving kitten they had once given a plate of milk. He ate the potatoes as greedily. When they were all gone, he wiped his mouth with the back of his hand and slouched down in the chair. Nelly wished that his nose was painted

red and his hair brushed forward so he wouldn't look so sad.

"Is the circus near here?" she asked hopefully.

"No," answered Fernand. "I got a ride with a truck driver coming this way." He looked furtively at Uncle Simon. "We are still trying to make both ends meet at the Fair, but we've had ill luck all winter. Bad weather is no help to carnivals. The fees are going up all the time. And Uncle Bruno paid a good price for that monkey. Then Noisette chewed a hole in a man's coat while he was watching our free outside show. So besides a free show from us, he got a free new coat too."

Uncle Simon was one to beat the hare out of the bush as soon as possible. "So my brothers want another loan," he put in tartly.

Aunt Barbe was indignant. "We work from dawn to dusk on this farm to make our living," she said. "And why should our horses and cow and fowl work to support a lot of useless animals that stand on balls and prance around on their hind legs instead of doing honest work?"

"It's keeping all those fancy creatures that is taking the money," said Uncle Simon. "I have told my brothers a dozen times that they should get rid of them and buy a merry-go-round. Have you ever seen an idle merry-go-round at a carnival?"

"A merry-go-round with *wooden* horses!" exclaimed Nelly in a shocked voice.

Fernand said quietly, "Perhaps to you, Uncle, your animals are only beasts to do your work. But to us in the circus business, they are performers like ourselves. They are like part of the family."

Aunt Barbe's eyes flashed. "I can tell you that our farm animals are part of the family too," she retorted. "Did I not sit up all night with the cow when she was sick? Do I not talk to my ducks and worry about my chickens when it rains?"

Uncle Simon backed her up. "Did we have Forte destroyed when he grew old and lame?" he asked.

Fernand smiled roguishly at them. "Then you understand why we can't sell the circus and why we must take care of *our* animals," he said smoothly. "So I know you will give us the loan we need."

Uncle Simon felt that he had been tricked, but he did not give up easily. "If you did so poorly this winter," he asked, "why do you expect things to be better from now on?"

Fernand leaned forward and the smile on his face broadened. He looked like the happy-go-lucky clown again. "Because we have arranged for a place at the big Gingerbread Fair that begins in Paris on Easter Saturday," he said. "That is, if we can raise the money for the fee and space rental."

Nelly and Marc began dancing with excitement.

"Then we can join the circus during the Easter holidays," shrieked Nelly. "You will be so close."

"We won't have to wait until summer," cried Marc.

Fernand nodded. Then to their delight he went into his funny pantomime of a man trying to swat a fly.

Uncle Simon and Aunt Barbe laughed at his antics too. Then they looked at the children's radiant faces. Uncle Simon rattled some coins in his pocket.

"We'll do it one more time, won't we, Barbe?" he asked his wife. "There's quite a sum now in that old tin box buried you-know-where."

"All right," agreed Aunt Barbe, "but this is the last time. Another failure and your brothers will have to sell their fancy animals and do some other kind of carnival work."

It was a terrible threat, but it did not worry Nelly too much. Already she had decided that she would think up such a clever act for Arabelle that the circus would make a fortune at the Gingerbread Fair in Paris.

She told Fernand about her goose and the lesson which had ended so badly.

"Don't you remember the sign painted on front of the

Petit Cirque Flandin?" her brother reminded her. " 'We train our animals with kindness and patience.' That is the only way."

"That's the way I trained Forte to harness," put in Uncle Simon as he began cleaning his pipe with a chestnut burr.

"And I trained the chickens to stay out of the kitchen," added Aunt Barbe, "but it wasn't with kindness and patience. It was with the broom."

They all laughed heartily and Aunt Barbe rose to take off the empty plates. Nelly helped her but hovered in the doorway as much as possible.

Fernand winked at her. "You better get that goose trained fast," he said, "because some new pupils are waiting for you. Nanette had twin kids this year and they're born performers."

"Can they stand on stilts or balance on a ball?" asked Marc.

"They can't stand on anything for two minutes," said Fernand. "All they do is jump through the air. And somebody has to watch them all the time they are loose because they have inherited their mother's good taste in clothes. But tell me. Just what are you going to teach Arabelle to do?"

Nelly's face fell. There were so many interesting things

that a goose could be taught. She could be taught to jump through a hoop or play dead or walk a tightrope—if she were only willing to learn.

"Begin with something simple," advised Fernand. "Perhaps she could pull a little wagon."

Uncle Simon rapped his pipe against the stove. "I wish she could pull my big wagon in case the other horse goes lame," he said.

"I'll be satisfied if she learns to lay eggs," said Aunt Barbe.

"Oh, any old goose can lay an egg," exclaimed Nelly.

"Arabelle hasn't laid one yet," Marc reminded her.

"That's because she isn't an ordinary goose," said Nelly. "She's going to be a great circus star, not an egg layer."

Aunt Barbe tightened her lips. "If those great circus stars of the Petit Cirque Flandin laid eggs or gave richer milk, Fernand wouldn't look thin as a rake," she said.

But Nelly didn't hear her words. She was the circus Nelly again, dressed in rustly satins and sparkling jewels, while high over her head Arabelle was swinging from a trapeze by one webbed foot.

Kindness and patience! Would she ever have enough to teach Arabelle to perform?

"It's easy to be kind to Arabelle," she said aloud, "but it's hard to be patient."

24

CHAPTER THREE

The Education of a Goose

Fernand had to leave early next morning to meet his truck-driver friend at the crossroads. He thanked Aunt Barbe and Uncle Simon as he swung his old canvas bag over his shoulder. He solemnly shook hands with Marc then kissed Nelly, first on one red cheek then the other. He repeated their messages to the rest of the family to show that he hadn't forgotten them.

His aunt and uncle wanted him to take a basket of eggs and a wheel of cheese with him for the family, but he refused. "Raoul's truck will be packed tight as a chestnut burr already," Fernand said. But he accepted a string of sausages that would go into his bag.

He tweaked Nelly's nose. "Kindness and patience," he

reminded her. "And if I have to wait around all morning for that Raoul and his truck, I'll thrash him."

Nelly made herself busy cleaning up the breakfast dishes. She helped unmake the beds and hang the bedding out of the windows to air. She even washed lettuce heads and leeks at the pump so they would be ready to sell in the market at St. Germain-en-Laye next day. But all the

time she was working so industriously, the other Nelly was training Arabelle.

"Steady now," she told a lettuce head, balancing it on the back of her hand. "Now jump through the hoop." She tossed the lettuce into the air. But she couldn't catch it. It fell on the ground and rolled in the dirt.

Nelly sighed and washed it again. She kept watching the gateway for Marc's return from an errand at the store.

Aunt Barbe came out and threw breakfast scraps to the chickens and ducks. "You will have to work harder and lay more eggs so we can support those worthless circus creatures," she said sharply. She paused at Forte's stable. "You must go out and work even if your leg is stiff," she said, "so we will have a bigger harvest and be able to feed those fancy ponies." She looked down the path to the cow pasture. "Mind," she called to the cow. "You must eat faster and make milk faster so those goats can spend all their time doing stunts at carnivals."

As Nelly listened to her aunt, her hands finished all their chores. But Marc wasn't home yet. He was probably turning somersaults for the storekeeper and his customers. She wanted him to help hitch Arabelle to his little wagon. She remembered that Fernand had suggested such a stunt.

At last she could wait no longer. She would teach Arabelle to jump rope. She looked for her skipping rope and coaxed the goose in front of her. "You must learn faster and work harder so the Flandin circus can go on," she echoed Aunt Barbe's words.

The chickens and ducks stopped their everlasting search for tidbits and gathered in a scattered circle around the two performers. The ducks were even a little jealous of Arabelle.

"Pe-e-ep," said a young hen peevishly.

Nelly readied herself and Arabelle for the jump.

"Now jump," she commanded Arabelle as she started the rope. But the goose didn't jump until the rope hit her tail. She gave an angry honk. She nipped at the rope then ran for the shed. From the safety of the old cart, she stuck her long neck out and eyed the rope as if it were a snake that had attacked her.

Nelly was angry. She burst into tears. At the same time Aunt Barbe came out of the kitchen.

"What's wrong?" asked her aunt. "Did you hurt yourself?"

"No," sobbed Nelly. "It's all Arabelle's fault. She's just a stupid goose. She won't do anything I try to teach her."

Aunt Barbe drew her lips together. "It's not natural for animals to do tricks," she said disapprovingly. "You're trying to make her go against her true nature."

They both looked up to see Marc coming through the

28

gate, carrying a string bag of grocery sacks and boxes. Marc was in high spirits.

"I did fifteen somersaults in succession at the store," he boasted, "and the storekeeper gave me a nougat bar." He proudly held up the candy. "I'll let you have a bite," he offered Nelly. "First we'll get my wagon and hitch up Arabelle," he cried as he handed the bag to Aunt Barbe. After his own success, he felt unusually generous toward his sister.

This should be easier for Arabelle, thought Nelly. Pull-

ing a wagon shouldn't be going against her nature too much even if she wasn't a horse.

Aunt Barbe went back into the kitchen to put the purchases away. Marc proudly brought out his little wagon from the truck shed. He had made it himself, using the wheels from an old baby carriage that a neighbor had given him. Uncle Simon had whittled the shafts and painted it a bright blue, like his own carts had been when they were new. There was no horse small enough to pull it so Marc thought it would be fun to see Arabelle between the shafts.

Nelly looked through the shed and found an old horse bridle hanging on a wooden peg. Arabelle came out from under the big cart and followed her to see what new stunt had been thought up.

The loop of bridle that should have gone around a horse's ears was dropped over Arabelle's head and came to rest on her snowy breast. The bit that should have gone in a horse's mouth was drawn under her tail. The strap that should have buckled under a horse's flat cheeks was fastened over her back. The harness didn't fit Arabelle very well but, after all, it had been made for a horse and not a goose. The little wagon fitted her better because the shafts were just the right distance apart for a fat goose to squeeze between them.

The children found some pieces of twine to make the

traces which fastened the harness to the cart.

"We'll let the old rooster have the first ride," said Nelly. She started toward him, but the cock who had always been such a crowing braggart was afraid. He fled to the hen house for protection. The ducks didn't want to ride either. They made for the path that led down the hill to their muddy pond in the cow pasture.

"Then I'll get my doll," said Nelly. "She loves to ride in a carriage. It isn't going against her nature at all."

The doll made no objection to the remarkable ride awaiting her. She didn't run away. She let Nelly put her best coat and bonnet on her. She leaned back fearlessly when Nelly set her in the blue wagon. The rooster returned to the audience and eyed the doll, but the ducks stayed away.

The children beamed with pride as they released Arabelle and stood back, admiring her and the bright cart with its well-dressed passenger. Arabelle looked as sturdy and dependable as old Forte. She peered back at the cart with awe as if to ask, "How did that ever grow out of my tail?" She twitched her tail to see if the wagon would twitch too.

Nelly stepped in front of her. She bowed to the bright-eyed chickens and a neighbor cat that had just jumped up on the wall. "Ladies and gentlemen," she announced, "Arabelle, the feathered steed, will now lead the grand parade around the ring."

31

"Ork," said the rooster with awe.

"Moo," came the cow's mournful voice from the pasture, as if she were begging admission to the show. One duck returned from the pond.

Nelly took a few steps backward. "Come," she called to Arabelle. But the goose stood stubbornly between the shafts. "Can't you see I'm tied down?" was what she may have thought.

"Giddap, Arabelle," ordered Nelly.

"Honk," said Arabelle, but that was all she did.

Nelly put her hands on her hips and frowned at the goose. "Don't you want to go to Paris and become a great circus star?" she asked.

"Honk," was Arabelle's only answer.

Marc gave the little wagon a gentle push, and Arabelle took one unwilling step forward.

"Ork," repeated the rooster, winking at Arabelle. The cat crouched on the wall, waiting.

Marc gave the wagon a hard shove which jolted the doll and almost swept Arabelle off her webbed feet.

"Honk, honk," the goose cried in alarm, as if this new tail were getting out of control. She tried to flap her wings but was more alarmed because the shafts kept them from flapping. Then she fled across the cobbles.

The wagon rattled and tugged behind her. The doll bounced from side to side without any dignity. This only terrified Arabelle the more. She thought the wagon was chasing her.

"Honk, honk, honk," she screamed as she raced around the courtyard madly, bumping the wagon first into the wall then against the stone watering trough. The chickens stampeded to the fowl yard like a circus audience in a panic over an escaped lion, and the cat disappeared behind the wall.

"My wagon!" cried Marc. "She's breaking my wagon!" One wheel had come off and a shaft had cracked.

"My doll!" screamed Nelly. "Whoa, Arabelle! Whoa!"

She ran to stop Arabelle, but the frightened goose shied like a skittish horse and made for the path that led to

the pasture. Another wheel fell off. The doll bounced furiously and so did the back of the wagon.

Down the path and into the muddy duck pond went Arabelle, and out of it flapped the quacking ducks when they found themselves right in the middle of the act.

Marc and Nelly were as wet and muddy as the goose by the time they dragged her out of the water. Only the doll had been saved from a bath because she had fallen out on the last bounce. She lay in a faint on the grass, her gown disarranged and her bonnet hanging on a stinging nettle.

Nelly rescued her doll and was glad to see that she wasn't broken. She helped the honking goose out of the harness. Marc stalked behind her, carrying what was left of his wagon. Nelly chased Arabelle ahead of her.

"Kindness and patience," she said loudly. "Kindness and patience. Kindness and patience." She chanted it over and over like a magic formula to keep herself from wringing Arabelle's neck.

"Oh, close your mouth," hissed Marc between clenched teeth. "If you say that once more, I'll wring Arabelle's neck."

They had to change their clothes, and Aunt Barbe made Nelly wash them immediately. She made Marc carry water from the pump and fill the big boiler. She made him carry in wood and build up a roaring fire to boil the water. She made him help Nelly lift the hot, dripping garments with a long pole from the steaming pan. Then an unhappier thought came to Marc. "The nougat bar," he cried. "It was in the pocket of my jacket. Now it's all cooked into the clothes."

When the clothes were hanging on the mended line, Aunt Barbe relented a little. She gave each of the children a big piece of bread.

They sat on a bench in the courtyard, munching their bread and trying to find forgiveness for Arabelle in their hearts. The goose was doing her own cleaning by spreading the feathers of her chest to dry them. She had already forgiven the children for any wrong they had done her. She waddled up to them and eyed Nelly's last bite of bread. "Honk," she begged.

Her honk was like a ray of light to Nelly. She jumped to her feet with new hope. "It's all our fault," she told Marc. "Remember how Papa and Odile train the animals? They give them something to eat. That's how they taught the ponies to walk on their hind legs and the goats to balance on the planks and stilts. And the dogs."

Marc rubbed his nose sheepishly. "They give them sugar and little pieces of meat," he added. "Why didn't we think of that before we let Arabelle break my wagon?"

Nelly gave the goose the last bite of bread. "I wonder

what else Arabelle would like to eat?" she asked. "I'm sure she doesn't care for sugar or meat. And Aunt Barbe won't let us waste good bread on a goose."

Then she remembered that Arabelle simply loved fresh leaves of any kind. So she ran into the pasture and picked the most tasty-looking dandelion leaves she could find.

By the time she returned, Marc had rigged up a plank on boxes for Arabelle to walk. Nelly thrust the dandelion greens into her pocket then Marc helped her to lift the

goose on top of a box. The chickens and ducks came slowly out of the fowl yard.

Nelly took up her position at the other end of the plank. She held out a dandelion leaf to the goose. "Come here, Arabelle," she tempted. "Come get your snack."

Arabelle stretched her neck but it wouldn't go all the way across the plank. "Honk, honk," she begged. She put one foot on the board.

"There she goes," cried Marc. "She's going to walk the plank."

Nelly nibbled at the dandelion leaf to show the goose how good it was. But Arabelle didn't trust the loose plank under her foot. She had a better idea. She honked hungrily, swooped to the ground, and waddled under the plank toward Nelly.

"Kindness and patience," said Nelly to herself again. They put Arabelle back on the box. Then Nelly waved the dandelion green back and forth in front of her.

Arabelle's head followed it from side to side. She rose on her toes and stepped from foot to foot in time with Nelly's hand. She flapped her wings gently. She raised them higher and flapped them harder. She raised them all the way over her head and flapped them wildly as she hopped from one foot to the other.

"She's dancing," cried Nelly with delight. "She's doing

a beautiful dance. Nelly, the graceful goose, is doing her dance of the swan."

"Ork, ork," cried the rooster, clapping his own wings against his sides as if in applause.

"Quack, quack," approved the ducks.

Nelly fed Arabelle the greens which her performance had won.

"She's a dancing goose," she said proudly. "No wonder she didn't want to pull a wagon or walk a plank. I'll make a fancy ballet costume for her and put a necklace around her throat. I'll glue some ostrich feathers in her tail. Oh, how people will clap!"

Marc was not impressed. "That's a crusty old act," he said. "I'm going to learn to do fifty somersaults in succession then they'll want to see *me*. I'm going to practice and practice even if I shake my ears loose from my head."

"Perhaps you are going against your true nature trying to do so many somersaults," suggested Nelly. "Maybe you should be a clown like Fernand."

CHAPTER FOUR

Market Day

The spring days seemed to pass by as slowly as the Hundred Years' War that Nelly was studying in her history book. She and Marc couldn't understand why the farm days were so long and the carnival days so short. However, their uncle and aunt were always complaining that the days weren't long enough for their work.

The children would eagerly ask any strange travelers if they had seen carnival caravans on the road. They asked truck drivers and tramps. They asked the man and woman who drove their store to the village twice a week. The store was a closed metal van like Uncle Simon's market truck. But the back doors cleverly opened and folded into a counter. Shelves full of aprons, blouses, and notions ran all around the inside.

"I saw a big carnival truck stuck on the hill above Marly," said the storeman, "and they'll get a heavy fine because they aren't supposed to use that route."

Nelly was worried. "Was it a train of two trucks and a house trailer with Petit Cirque Flandin written on the sides?" she asked.

The storekeepers shook their heads vaguely. They weren't really interested in any truck but their own.

Nelly was so impatient that she even tried to make time go faster by working harder than ever around the house and farmyard. Perhaps she could shorten the day in Aunt Barbe's way.

Suddenly, just overnight, the school days were ended and the first week of vacation began. A postcard had come from the town of Angers saying that the children were to join the circus in Paris the Thursday before Easter. Marc and Nelly argued over who should have the postcard with its picture of a ruined castle.

Aunt Barbe settled the quarrel. "The card is addressed to me," she told Nelly, "but if you let Marc have it, you may go with me tomorrow to sell our vegetables in the market at St. Germain-en-Laye. Your uncle's rheumatism has been bothering him so I think he should take a rest for once from that damp, cold market place. I can drive the truck as well as he. A truck is no different from a horse. You just have to show it who is master."

This proposal met with the children's approval. Nelly had never gone to the market and Marc preferred to stay home and practice somersaults. Twice a week Uncle Simon and Aunt Barbe filled the truck with vegetables and baskets of eggs and drove grandly through the archway.

"May Arabelle go too?" begged Nelly. "She really should get used to crowds so she won't be shy performing at the carnival."

Aunt Barbe agreed, but made the rule that the goose would have to travel in a big basket.

Nelly had to get up before dawn the next morning. She helped load the truck by the dim electric light that hung in the shed. She put Arabelle in the old basket and squeezed it among the boxes of leeks and carrots and lettuce and the basket of eggs.

Aunt Barbe truly drove the truck as well as her husband, although she kept shouting "whoa" and "giddap" to it. But it knew that she was master.

Nelly sat inside where she could be with Arabelle. It was much like traveling in the trailer house of the Petit Cirque Flandin. She stood up from time to time and looked through the oval window in the back door. She wished

41

it wasn't so foggy outside. She couldn't tell whether any of the honking cars were carnival trucks or not.

She was thrilled when Aunt Barbe drove the truck over the cobbled streets of St. Germain-en-Laye and past the great, rounded walls and balconied roof of the ancient royal palace.

They reached the market square when the big clock on the post office said seven o'clock. The stalls of the market, with their canvas roofs and wooden tables, had already been set up by the market workers and many trucks were unloading in the fog.

"Whoa!" Aunt Barbe ordered. "This is our place."

Like the farm horses, the truck came to an obedient stop. Nelly helped her aunt lift the boxes and baskets out and arrange the vegetables in neat piles. Lastly she took the scales and their little weights out of a small scarred chest.

She dragged Arabelle's basket under the table while Aunt Barbe drove the truck away to park it. "I'll have to find a hitching place on a side street," explained her aunt, "so it won't block traffic."

On one side of the Flandin stall was an old lady selling work aprons and frilly underwear. On the other was a man with his wife presiding over beautiful bouquets and pots of flowers.

43

Across was a stall filled with all kinds of garden produce. The man behind the table was calling his wares in a loud, hoarse voice. He argued and coaxed people into buying his beets and turnips whether they wanted them or not.

When he thought that it was time to sell something else, he picked up a head of cauliflower. "Choice cabbage flower here," he cried. He banged it against the counter with all his might to show what solid cauliflower it was. "You can't do that to your own heads," he boasted to the women shoppers with their string bags and trundle baskets. Next he bowed over the turnips. "They may not be as pretty as those flowers over there," he cried, "but they taste much better."

Nelly was nettled by all the man's bragging about the produce he was selling.

"I have a goose that can dance," she called across to him.

"Ha, little one!" answered the man. "I have carrots that can dance. Just drop them in your soup kettles, mesdames, and they will dance like hares in the moonlight."

Nelly pouted and tossed her long hair back. She jumped from her high stool and took Arabelle out of the basket. The goose winked at the greenery and the flowers next door, and greedily snapped her beak. Nelly plucked a leaf from a head of lettuce. She waved it back and forth in front

44

of Arabelle's yellow beak. The goose turned one eye to the leaf. Back and forth she leaned on her webbed feet. Then she stretched her wings and raised them over her body. Higher and higher she raised them as she honked and flapped. She was performing for her first real audience, because curious shoppers were gathering at the stall to watch the unusual sight.

Aunt Barbe hurriedly pushed her way through the crowd because she thought some accident had happened

to Nelly. When she saw what was going on, she was quick to take advantage of it.

"Lettuce, mesdames," cried Aunt Barbe in her loudest voice, the one she usually saved for Forte. "Our lettuce is so young and tender that fowl dance for it."

The rival market man across the way was furious, because people who should have been buying his produce were gathering around the other stall. He dropped the cauliflower in his hand and picked up a purple eggplant left over from the winter.

"Look at this," he shouted. "Can any goose lay such a beautiful egg? And only a franc apiece."

But no one wanted to buy an eggplant for a franc when he could watch a goose dance for nothing.

Then an old man with a muffler wrapped around his head decided that this wasn't fair. He threw a franc at the feet of the dancing goose. A woman whose bag was too full to hold any more vegetables promptly tossed some leftover change to the goose. Soon a rain of coins sent Arabelle squawking to safety under the counter.

The man across the way dropped his eggplant on the purple mound. He slowly counted out five shining francs. Then he beckoned to Nelly. "I will give you these if you will stop showing off your goose and put her away in the basket," he said.

Nelly accepted the money although it puzzled her that Arabelle should make so much without any effort at all. But the goose still gained attention. A St. Germain merchant on his way to the post office stooped under the table and poked Arabelle.

"I'll give you twenty-five francs for that fat goose," he offered Aunt Barbe.

"Oh, no," cried Nelly in alarm. "She's a trained goose."

The man was disappointed. "I wanted her for my Easter dinner," he explained. "Such a fat goose would look charming stuffed with sauerkraut and garnished with sausages in the Alsatian way."

"No, indeed!" cried Nelly indignantly. "Arabelle is too special."

She shuddered to think of her pet's fate if she were an ordinary goose in Alsace. She was frightened to think of what awaited all the trained Flandin animals if the circus went broke. Then she confidently relaxed. Arabelle had proven that she could make money for the Petit Cirque Flandin and keep the animals in their jobs. She could even make money by not dancing.

Nelly counted the francs. Twelve of them. Already Arabelle was making money for the Flandins and she hadn't even joined the circus yet.

It was one o'clock by the post-office clock so Aunt Barbe

47

began bringing things out of the lunch basket—slices of ham, cheese, and sweet butter. "And run down to the other end of the square and buy us some fresh hot bread," she told Nelly, carefully counting out some coins from the cigar box beside the scales. "We'll eat lunch as we sell to the stragglers, then we'll pack up and go home. It has been a good day."

"It has been a wonderful day," cried Nelly. She ran through the little alleys of the market and found the bakery with its fresh, hot loaves. She bought something else as she returned through the market, using the money Arabelle had earned. She stopped at a fruit stall and bought Aunt Barbe a pear whose stem was artistically wrapped in tin foil. She yearned to buy herself an orange from Provence or an apple from Normandy, but she didn't want to spend any more of Arabelle's money. She was going to save it to buy the goose a dancing costume.

She ate her lunch so fast that Aunt Barbe gave her permission to look in the store windows along the nearby streets. In a narrow street running toward the castle, she found the loveliest eye-feast of all. It was a candy store whose windows were crowded with gilded nests of candy eggs, white fur swans carrying Easter eggs on their backs, chocolate hens, and beribboned bunnies.

It reminded her of how close was Easter and the Gingerbread Fair and Paris and the Flandins. She clinked the coins in her pocket. The Easter goodies were so tempting, but she tore herself away from the windows. She wanted to save the rest of the money for Arabelle's costume.

She had heard of the famous dressmakers in Paris. Perhaps one of them would make Arabelle a beautiful gown for the eleven francs left. She could see Arabelle preening herself before gold-framed mirrors while a stylish dressmaker pinned ruffles of tulle under her wings and draped flounces of net around her tail. She could almost hear all the little seamstresses exclaiming, *"Oh, là, là!* What style! What elegance!"

CHAPTER FIVE

On the Road to Paris

It was a few days later that Nelly and Marc had their first glorious proof that the Gingerbread Fair would soon open in Paris.

They were returning from the nearby woods, where Nelly had gathered bluebells and cuckoo flowers and Marc had chosen just the right piece of elder branch to carve himself a whistle. Nelly's quick eye caught sight of a small green and red truck pulling a trailer house down the road. The caravan slowed when it came abreast of the children. Tacked up on the side of the house on wheels was a blue poster showing a jolly girl in a yellow dress eating a candy cane as she sat sideways on a big pink pig. GINGERBREAD FAIR AT PARIS said the bold letters in the background.

Marc shouted and pointed, and both of them were delighted when the truck coughed to a stop. Nelly ran to the man driving it.

"Are you going to the Gingerbread Fair?" she cried. "Have you seen the Petit Cirque Flandin trucks? Will you see the circus as soon as you get there? Will you tell Mama and Papa that we're coming as soon as we can?"

But the man had his own question he wanted answered

DAVIS COUNTY PUBLIC LIBRARY
KAYSVILLE, UTAH

first. "Can you tell me the way to Paris?" he asked. "I took the wrong road somewhere."

Marc was more than ready to help him. "You turn left at the second road," he directed. "Then you drive on until you come to Madame Pingle's house. Take a right turn around Madame then you'll come to Monsieur Martin's sugar-beet field. There's a road that goes off there but don't take it because you'll end up in the field."

"It's real muddy, too, so you'll get stuck," put in Nelly. "There's another road farther down but don't take that one either. Keep on going until you reach the pasture with two cows in it."

The man put his hands over his ears and made a sad face. "Hush, hush," he implored. "You have me more lost than ever. Isn't there a simpler way to get to Paris?"

"You can keep on this road and it will take you right there," said Marc, "but it's longer."

The man decided he would take the longer and surer road. Then he answered some of the children's eager questions. No, he hadn't seen the Petit Cirque Flandin. Yes, he was going to the Gingerbread Fair and a great one it would be this year. There would be at least five hundred booths and his daughter expected to be crowned the Esmeralda of the carnival.

"What kind of a booth do you have?" asked Nelly, because his outfit looked too small to be carrying a merry-go-round or a circus.

"I sell Papa's beard," said the man. "You should see how much I sold at the Fair of St. Michael in Le Havre! Clouds of it. Everybody loves Papa's beard." The children agreed that nothing tasted better than the colored cotton candy swirled around a stick. "Come to see me at the Fair," he invited, "and I'll give you some free."

Then he ground the starter, the whole truck throbbed, the trailer house jerked, and the gay yellow girl went riding her pig down the longer road to Paris.

That evening Uncle Simon explained to them why the pink pig was the symbol of the carnival. "St. Anthony is the patron of swineherds," he said, "and gingerbread was first made at his abbey that once stood in the part of Paris where the Fair is held."

"Why?" asked Nelly.

Uncle Simon explained that there was history connected with the gingerbread, but Nelly did not mind that kind of history. "In the tenth century," he explained, "there was a great famine in the villages of Picpus, Montreuil, and Vincennes, which are now part of Paris. There was no wheat for bread and little of anything else, so the good monks of St. Anthony made up a bread of rye and honey to feed the people. That's how gingerbread was first made.

Each year since then, a fair has been held to celebrate the event."

"Those people were lucky to get gingerbread instead of regular bread," said Marc.

"We're luckier," said Nelly, "because we get to go to the big fair and that candy man said that it would be the best one ever."

"And I like Papa's beard even better than gingerbread," admitted Marc. "When will we leave for the Fair, Aunt Barbe?"

"That makes a problem for me like the famine did for the monks," answered his aunt. "I can't leave your uncle long enough to take you to Paris. His rheumatism is so bad that he needs my help. We are trying to find a ride for you."

For a few days the children were frightened that they would have no way to get to Paris to join the family. Easter was not far away and already part of their vacation was gone.

The couple who drove the store truck were willing to drive them to the Fair until they found out that Arabelle would be a passenger too.

"A dog or even a well-raised and reasonable cat we could have in our neat store," said the woman, "but not a messy goose."

Nelly quickly explained that Arabelle would be in a basket, but the woman still refused. "We have never carried geese in our store," she insisted. "It is a dry-goods truck not a poultry wagon."

When the children were full of despair and Nelly had cried her eyes red, a kindly farmer who was taking a load of pigs to the slaughterhouse in the Villette district of Paris offered to drive them to the very Place du Trône where the Fair would be held.

"If you don't mind riding with my pigs," said the farmer.

"Oh, I'd love to go there with pigs," cried Nelly, feeling like the gay yellow girl riding the pink pig to the Fair. "But may Arabelle go too?"

"If my pigs don't object, why should I?" asked the farmer. "And who are my pigs to object to a goose?"

It was in the early morning that they set out for Paris with the children's belongings packed into two market bags. Arabelle in her basket was placed among the pigs. Marc and Nelly climbed up into the cab with the farmer. Aunt Barbe squeezed in a big wheel of cheese for the family. Arabelle stuck her long neck out of the basket and hissed at the pigs, but they did not object to her at all. Then the pigs squealed and the farmer gaily honked his horn for half a kilometer down the road.

"*Allô,* Paris! *Bonjour,* Paris!" he sang in time to his horn. "Make room for us because here we come."

The children squealed as shrilly as the pigs, Arabelle honked as loudly as the horn, and the truck raced down the road to Madame Pingle's house, went around Madame and past Monsieur Martin's sugar-beet field until it reached the pasture with the two cows—only the cows weren't in it because they were shut up in the barn.

They joined the traffic on the main road to Paris, but there was a stop to be made as the farmer wanted a bite of food at a little restaurant. The Relais of the Golden Pheasant was a friendly roadside place with tables out in the open air and a carefree vine growing over a trellis.

"Tra-la-la, tra-lee-lee," sang the farmer, honking his horn again for musical accompaniment. "It's time to eat, eat, eat. Come in," he invited the children, "and I'll buy you each a ham sandwich. Eating ham creates a demand for pigs."

They sat at a table shaded by the vine and Nelly watched a woman pick out a special table and seat her white poodle on the chair across from her. The woman scanned the menu and was very particular when she ordered how a beefsteak was to be cooked. "And bring a bottle of Evian water," she ordered the waiter.

As Nelly and Marc munched their ham sandwiches, the waiter brought a medium-rare steak on a platter and set it before the woman.

"No, no," she told him, "it is for Frisette and please cut it up for her. The water is for me."

The poodle sniffed the steak disdainfully and turned her black nose up in the air. Then the cook himself came out in his tall white cap and white apron. He crossed his arms and frowned at Frisette so fiercely that she began eating her meat.

Nelly tried to make her sandwich last a long time so

she could watch the poodle eating so daintily. The farmer finished his sandwich in three bites then went to talk to the proprietor near his truck.

The children saw him take one of the pigs from the truck and point out its merits to the restaurant owner.

"No," said the owner. "It's the goose I want."

Nelly quickly joined them to tell him that the goose was not for sale, even as she had told the merchant in the market of St. Germain-en-Laye. To prove it she brought Arabelle out of her basket and had her dance by the table, although the snobbish poodle refused to look.

"It's ham sandwiches you sold just now," said the farmer, "not goose sandwiches. A pig would be a better buy."

A big, shiny automobile slowed down and two tourists stared at the Relais of the Golden Pheasant.

"Oh, let's eat at this quaint little place with all the animals," exclaimed the woman.

The man grunted. "If you want to eat with animals, it would be quainter to have a picnic lunch in some farmer's barnyard," he retorted. But he stopped the motor and helped the woman out of the car.

The proprietor carried the squealing pig into his restaurant. The tourists argued over whether to sit in the sun or the shade. The lady at the table wiped Frisette's mouth fastidiously with the napkin. Arabelle was put back into the basket. The farmer jingled the coins in his pocket and madly honked the horn as he started to sing again.

"Oh, Paris, here we come," he sang. "Open that Arc de Triomphe wide, wide, wide."

A gray haze, faint as breath on a mirror, hung over Paris. But the children did not get to see the Arc de Triomphe because the truck took a short cut. They did see the Eiffel Tower rising over the magic city like a spire of dark lace and high hope.

"Isn't it wonderful?" cried Nelly, squeezing Marc's arm. "This is the happiest day of my life."

"Honk! Honk!" cried Arabelle in agreement.

"Oink! Oink!" squealed the pigs dismally, because it certainly wasn't the happiest day in their lives.

Nelly looked back at them sympathetically. "If only you had taught them to dance on their hind legs," she told the farmer, "you could be taking them to the Fair instead of the slaughterhouse."

The farmer jingled the money in his pockets again. "One and two and three!" he sang as he started to blow his horn. "Step, hop, step! My pigs shall dance to the market so I can dance at the Fair."

Then in fright he hurriedly turned down a side street because he suddenly remembered that it is against the law for a motorist to blow his horn in Paris.

They drove down the winding street and came out at a busy intersection where a policeman was helping people to cross on foot. He motioned the truck to stop.

"Honk, honk," complained Arabelle loudly.

The policeman scowled at the truck and started toward them, pulling a pad out of his pocket.

"Honking horns in Paris is forbidden," he sternly told the farmer.

"It wasn't the horn," protested the farmer. "It was one of my passengers."

The policeman took a turn scowling at the pigs.

"Oink, oink," they sassed him.

He began to write on his pad. Arabelle stretched her neck over the seat toward him. She frowned back at him with one eye.

"Honk, honk," she objected.

The policeman looked at her then put his pad back in his pocket. "Get along," he motioned. "There is no law against geese honking in Paris."

CHAPTER SIX

The Gingerbread Fair

The Gingerbread Fair was as great as the Candy Man had predicted. It was sprawled all along the three-laned avenue between the Place du Nation and the Porte de Versailles. The entrance was a copy of the old abbey of St. Anthony, with keeps and walls of plaster painted brown and blue. As far as the eye could see was an endless midway of gaudy stalls, side shows, and merry-go-rounds in all stages of construction.

Packed closely behind them were villages of the trucks and trailers of the carnival people. The Flandins had been lucky in coming early because the space allotted to them included a city bench next to their house on wheels. By adding their own table and a couple of rickety chairs, they had an outdoor dining room under the chestnut trees, which were raising green umbrellas.

Mama's geraniums were blooming in the flower boxes below the windows of the home on wheels. The back doors were opened wide and the set of steps fastened in place. At the other end of the house, a big red truck was parked and it made neighing, baaing, and barking sounds.

Nelly and Marc rushed to Mama, because she was the heart of the family. They hugged her and kissed her and told her they never wanted to leave her again.

"Honk, honk," Arabelle interrupted them, because she felt she should be introduced.

"What a fine, intelligent-looking goose!" exclaimed Mama. "She will have plenty of playmates."

"She's a real circus performer," said Nelly. "She's going to be our star."

"I can turn twenty-five somersaults," put in Marc.

"You must see Nanette's new kids," said Mama. "They're in the truck with the ponies and Dodo, because he's the watchdog."

"I can turn twenty-five somersaults, one right after another," repeated Marc.

"The other dogs are somewhere around," said Mama. "They've already found the food stalls."

63

"Mama, I can turn twenty-five somersaults," said Marc for the third time.

Mama hugged him again. "That is splendid," she said. "Papa will let you help with the free performance in front."

"But I'm too good to be free," protested the boy.

"We all have to do a few free acts to attract a crowd," said Mama. "And heaven knows we need all the customers we can get. Isn't that true, Odile?"

Their sister had just arrived from shopping. She dropped her basket and pushed back her tangle of long, curly hair as if in great surprise. "Who are these big children?" she asked. "What are they doing in our house? I've never seen them before."

"I'm Nelly," cried her little sister. She threw her arms around Odile.

"And I'm Marc," said the boy, but he didn't hug his big sister because he felt too old for such foolishness. "I can turn twenty-five somersaults."

"Honk, honk," put in Arabelle, as if to say, "I'm a big goose now, and wait until you see what I can do. I wouldn't spoil it by telling you."

"That's great," said Odile, "and can you hang by your toes from a trapeze, Nelly?"

Nelly shook her brown hair. "I'm a trainer," she said.

"I've been one ever since I broke Aunt Barbe's clothes-line."

"I'm a trainer too," said Odile, then she whispered, "but I think I'm going to be something else." She did a graceful, twirling dance step. "I think I'm going to be crowned the Esmeralda of the carnival this year."

Nelly remembered the Candy Man and his prediction that his own daughter would be chosen. She was worried that Odile might be disappointed.

"What is an Esmeralda?" she asked.

Odile laughed and tugged lightly at Nelly's earring. "She was a character thought up by the famous writer Victor Hugo," she explained. "Esmeralda was the Gypsy girl in his book called *Notre Dame de Paris*. She had a pet white goat and she danced to entertain the crowds in front of the cathedral of Notre Dame. That's why the carnival queen is called Esmeralda—because she's the favorite of people who make their living by entertaining."

Nelly was relieved. Odile would surely be chosen. Who else had a pet white goat like Nanette?

The children ran around front to where Papa, Uncle Bruno, and Fernand were setting up the circus theater. They had already laid the foundation of planks, high enough for the animals to stable under the floor. And the front partition had been set in place.

There was more hugging and kissing, and Uncle Bruno, who was also something of an artist, pointed proudly to the decorations on the front wall. He had painted pictures of the circus the way they all wished it to look inside instead of the way it really did. In a vast

arena, horses raced with Roman chariots, a dozen dogs
were performing all at once, and a herd of goats gam-
boled on mountain peaks. There was even a cat dancing
to the music of an orchestra of seals, but the cat had run
away because the carnival noises made her nervous, and
there had never been any seals.

"You can scrape off the cat and draw a goose instead,"
said Nelly proudly. "My Arabelle is a dancer." She
proudly read the sign that said the animals had been
trained with kindness and patience. "And that's how I
taught her to dance," she said.

Nelly looked around for Arabelle, but there wasn't a
feather of her in sight. She ran back to the trailer house,
but Mama hadn't seen the goose for some time. Nelly
was frightened. She knew that Paris was a great city and
no place for a lost goose even if the police wouldn't
arrest her for honking.

Nelly looked under trailer props and truck wheels.
The Gypsy fortune-teller next door was sitting beside
her booth peeling potatoes so Nelly asked her if she had
seen a goose.

"I see them every day and tell their fortunes," replied
the dark woman, "but I haven't seen one in feathers.
For two francs I will look in my crystal ball and tell
you where she is."

But Nelly didn't want to spend any of Arabelle's wardrobe money unless she was unable to find her anywhere but in a crystal ball.

She asked the Gingerbread Man across the way if he had seen a goose. He shook his head. He looked over all his gingerbread cookies, which were shaped like pigs to honor St. Anthony. They were luscious pigs frosted with red roses or white lilies of the valley.

"I don't see anything but pigs," said the Gingerbread Man. "I even see them in my sleep." He pointed to a sign hanging over his stall. It was also shaped like a pig and read, "We baptize them in a minute."

"Tell me your name," said the man, "and I will frost it on a pig for you while you wait."

Nelly thanked him but politely refused. She wouldn't dream of spending Arabelle's money on a pig even if it was named for her.

Then a man who was putting the finishing touches on a little building something like the Petit Cirque Flandin beckoned to her. He was a small, wiry man—"all bone and gristle" Uncle Simon would have said.

"Is it a big white honking bird you've lost?" he asked in a voice coated with the rich butter of Normandy. "She's back of that pile of boards visiting my monkeys."

He helped Nelly climb over some boards then led her

to his trailer. Arabelle was standing just beyond reach of five monkeys chained to the steps. Four of them were brown and the liveliest one gray, and they all had soft brown eyes. They were making faces to entertain Arabelle and the goose was honking back in applause.

Nelly was overjoyed at finding Arabelle. And she was charmed by the friendly little monkeys.

"What do they do?" she asked the man from Normandy.

"They really don't do anything," he confessed. "I fasten them in little racing cars and work a pedal that makes the cars run around on a platform. Then I give the winner—of course I give each one a turn at winning—a bit of carrot or celery. So the audience thinks the monkeys have done something marvelous, and so do the monkeys."

He showed Nelly the little uniforms the monkeys wore when they were racing.

"They're pretty old and dirty," he admitted, "but the monkeys think they look fine in them. Come out front again and let me show you the picture of the race."

He led Nelly to the front of his attraction again and proudly pointed to a scene of monkeys racing big cars around a speedway while thousands of onlookers applauded. No chains or straps held the monkeys so they were performing all kinds of antics. One stood on his head on the motor and another hung over the side of his car by his long tail. Like Uncle Bruno, the Monkey Man had made the scene look as he wished it did, because he added, "Of course it isn't that big and the cars don't have wheels because they run in grooves."

"I can hardly wait to see them," exclaimed Nelly. Her face fell. "But I can't spend my money looking at other shows. I have to use it to buy a costume for Arabelle."

"I don't intend to charge you," said the Monkey Man in a hurt voice. "After all, we are in the same business."

Nelly was proud of his words and happy that she had found an understanding friend so soon. "I want to have some famous dressmaker here in Paris design a costume for Arabelle," she confided.

The Monkey Man rubbed his unshaven chin thoughtfully. "How much money do you have to invest?" he asked.

"Eleven francs," said Nelly, "and Arabelle made it all by herself at the market in St. Germain-en-Laye. She made most of it by dancing, but she was paid some for not dancing."

Then she had to explain to the man why a goose that was such a fine dancer was paid to stop dancing.

"Eleven francs," said the man. "You couldn't even buy a handkerchief in those high-fashion salons for that. Now the place to go is the Flea Market. You'll find real bargains there."

"What is the Flea Market?" asked Nelly doubtfully, because it sounded like a place where one went to buy fleas, and the animals certainly didn't need any more of them.

"You've never heard of the Flea Market?" asked the man in surprise. "It's a famous old second-hand market held up in the northern part of Paris. Started in the way-back days when the vendors sold their stuff out there to save paying the taxes for bringing it into Paris proper. And they're still selling the same old stuff, I'll vow."

"How can I get there?" asked Nelly. "The Fair starts day after tomorrow."

"Just come with me that morning," said the man. "I

need to buy a new saw—that is, a new old saw. This one is so rusted and bent out of shape it's no use to me or a monkey."

Nelly clapped her hands and Arabelle honked. "I'll ask my mama," she cried.

"I'll ask her for you," he offered. "We're old friends. Your papa loaned me Dodo when one of my monkeys came down with the flu in Toulouse."

Nelly was eager to explore the rest of the Fair. She penned Arabelle in the big red truck with the ponies and the goats.

"Before you run off to play," Mama said to her and Marc, "you must carry some water from the hydrant at the corner. You're getting big enough to help with the work now. Your job will be to keep us in water." She gave a pail to each of them and pointed out the way.

Marc and Nelly made their meandering path around caravans and among loose chickens and their little peepers. They stepped over the electric cables of the huge power trucks. They found the hydrant easily because other people were using it too.

Dutifully they lugged the heavy pails back through the crooked path between the trucks and caravans.

As Mama poured the water into a big tub, the children started away.

"Wait!" called Mama. "This is just enough for the house. Fill these again and the empty ones under the truck for the animals. They must be out of drinking water."

The children filled the pails again then groaned at sight of the four empty ones under the truck.

"I don't see how they can be so thirsty," sighed Marc.

"I'm glad we don't have any elephants," added Nelly.

"And I'm gladdest we don't have all those seals Uncle Bruno painted," said Marc. "I bet they'd need a swimming pool."

"I guess circus life is harder than we thought," added Nelly, "but I don't care because I'm really home."

But when they walked down the long midway, they saw that everyone else was working even harder, nailing boards and shining metal work so the carnival would be ready by Saturday.

A man had put together the frame of his merry-go-round and was carrying the wooden horses out of his truck, one by one. A man and woman who ran a shooting gallery were hanging up clay pipes and ducks. Many of the food stalls were already doing a rush business. They were selling waffles, pancakes, and fritters to the carnival people and the idlers. Three little carnival girls wearing red shoes were buying gingerbread pigs.

There was also bustle in the abbey of St. Anthony, where more stands were being erected by men dressed in monks' brown robes.

Nelly turned her eyes up and saw the two tall monuments, each topped by an impressive statue.

"Who are they, Brother?" she politely asked a monk. All the men began to guffaw.

"They're kings," answered the one she had questioned. "Louis IX and Philippe Auguste, but I'm no monk so you don't have to call me 'Brother.'"

Nelly reddened with embarrassment.

"We're false monks," said another, "but our gingerbread is good as the real monks used to make."

Nelly quickly got over her embarrassment. She looked at the high statues, the false abbey of St. Anthony with its false monks, and the busy carnival midway.

"Oh, I hope the circus will make a lot of money so we can keep the animals," she told Marc fervently. "And I hope our acts will be so good that Mama and Papa will keep *us*."

CHAPTER SEVEN

The Flea Market

The Flandin circus was all put together by noon next day. It was made of a high stage with benches grouped in a small space below.

"We don't need much room for the audience because it is never very big," said Uncle Bruno. "But ha! You should see the crowd that gathers outside to watch the free show. Standing room only."

There were platforms along the front for the free performances and a little ticket coop where Mama would preside because she was good with money.

The goats and ponies were tethered under the stage so they could have some fresh air. The dogs and the kids ran loose, but Papa warned Marc and Nelly to keep an eye on the kids to see that they didn't eat anybody's clothes. Nelly resolved that she would keep an even sharper eye on them after Arabelle's gown was bought. She could hardly wait until the next day to select it at the Flea Market. She wanted it in time for Arabelle's first appearance.

The Flandins took turns rehearsing their acts. Fernand didn't bother to redden his nose or comb his hair forward, but he was so funny anyway that the children were convulsed with laughter. The goats and ponies acted like the old troupers they were, although they often had to repeat their tricks before they did them right. But Arabelle was perfect from beginning to end. She danced all around the stage, honking her own accompaniment even though Uncle Bruno had put a cracked record on the old-fashioned phonograph.

Nelly imagined her with lace ruffles and silken flounces billowing around her yellow legs.

"She really needs a costume," Uncle Bruno said. "I've seen geese dance like that in a barnyard, but never wearing skirts."

Nelly looked offended because Uncle Bruno considered Arabelle's act an ordinary farm sight.

"We put little dresses on the dogs, you know," Papa

77

cajoled her. "It adds what people call illusion. Makes the little creatures seem human."

Nelly thought the dogs' dresses were too soiled and rumpled to add much illusion. So she washed them that afternoon and even begged some starch from Mama. She hung them on a line across the truck door, and any passer-by might have thought that a family of elves lived inside. Then she sharpened her eyes on the kids to see that they didn't make a meal off the washing. Although the string was high, those kids were so clever at climbing that there was no telling what heights they might reach.

When the elfin dresses were almost dry, Nelly carefully ironed them. She was so pleased by the stiff, starchy appearance of the dogs' clothes that she decided to iron Odile's silk blouse, which had been brought out of a trunk for the opening performance. Everything went well until she heard the kids playing on the steps. They were climbing to the highest one then jumping off in great leaps like children showing off.

As Nelly watched them, a burning smell came to her nose. In horror she ran back to the shelf on which she had been ironing. The smoking iron was sitting on Odile's blouse. Nelly grabbed it up, but it was too late. There was a big brown mark on the back of the blouse.

Nelly wept and wept. "I'll use Arabelle's money to buy you a blouse at the Flea Market," she sobbed to her sister.

Odile had been very angry at first, but her little sister's grief made her relent. "Don't cry, Nelly," she finally consoled her. "I won't turn my back to the audience. And they'll be watching the goats anyway."

All the way to the Flea Market with the Monkey Man next day, Nelly thought about the burned blouse. Perhaps there would be enough money left over to buy Odile another blouse. How could she be Esmeralda with a big brown burn on her back?

They drove down streets lined with gray buildings

like layers of oyster shells. Nelly enjoyed looking at the crowds of people and the busy stores. She missed the jolly company of the singing farmer and his pigs. But the Monkey Man turned out to be an even more interesting companion because he knew so much about training animals. He told her that wild boars were easily trained if taken young but that a rabbit makes a poor pupil because it has little memory.

"I even knew a man who broke a cow to bridle and saddle," he told her. "Rode her around the ring and jumped her over low hurdles." Nelly wondered what Aunt Barbe might have to say about that.

The buildings grew shabbier, the streets narrower, and the crowds greater. A bazaar of stalls filled the sidewalks. A man came walking over the cobbles carrying a chair on his head. The stuffing was bursting from the seat and hung around his head like coarse, frizzled hair. Not far behind him trudged a woman carrying a stuffed badger that, in turn, carried a wooden umbrella rack.

"We are getting close to the Flea Market," remarked the Monkey Man.

He parked his car in a space between a motorcycle and a truck. Nelly hopped out and followed him through the market bazaar. He suddenly stopped and led her into a narrow cobbled alley. She stared at the booths on each side. It looked as if all the trash from the attics and cellars of Paris had been swept into them.

"Some folks' trash is the treasure of others," said the Monkey Man as they entered the maze of the Flea Market.

There was everything for sale that one could think of—and a lot of things that no one would have thought of, such as a suit of rusted chain armor, a spinning wheel, and a mummy case.

It was so crowded that Nelly walked many steps clinging to the hand of a strange man. Suddenly she and the man looked at each other in surprise. Then the Monkey Man came back to her and the strange man went off to find his own child.

"As you can see," said the Monkey Man, "the market is full of wonders at second hand. You may find a shawl once worn by the Empress Josephine or Marie Antoinette's petticoat for your goose."

They looked over the wares at each counter. Sometimes the Monkey Man found a rusty tool in a pile of junk. "No better than my own saw," he would say, tossing it back.

Nelly was overawed at the glass cases filled with perfume bottles, jewelry, and gewgaws of another age. She admired a huge copy of the famous painting of Mona

Lisa because the new artist had improved on the first picture by giving his lady a broad, friendly grin. Her eyes popped wide at the sight of two dried elephant feet that had been made into baskets. They popped even wider at the voodoo masks hanging over the head of a vendor who calmly ate a bowl of stew in spite of their baleful stares.

At one stand she was spellbound by a large glass music box which was tinkling a tune. The inside works were of silver, and tiny silver bees on wands daintily struck the notes. But the price written on a card beside the box ran into many figures. Oh, when Arabelle's act made the circus rich, she would come back to the market and buy the lovely music box to use in place of the wheezy phonograph.

"There it is," suddenly cried the Monkey Man. "The high fashion of your great-grandmother's day."

Immediately she saw the booth whose counters were piled high with faded satin, torn net, moth-eaten velvet, and grimy, bejeweled gowns. What a feast they would have offered the kids! Nelly eagerly rushed ahead. She stopped and ran her eyes and hands over the old clothes. Then she noticed more of them hanging in back of the booth. She stared at a ball gown of purple silk trimmed with crushed scarlet roses and green beads. The silk and roses were faded but the beads were bright as new. If only it were the right size for Arabelle. But how foolish! She could cut it up and perhaps there would still be enough for a blouse for Odile.

The market woman was dressed in a shiny black serge dress that looked as if her own grandmother might have worn it for her lifetime. As she knitted a heel into a sock, she furtively watched Nelly.

"How much is that beautiful purple gown?" asked the child.

The woman dropped her knitting at once. In the wink of an eye she had pulled the dress down and was dancing it before Nelly's enraptured eyes.

"Forty francs," said the woman. "And as good as new. Look at all the material in the skirt alone. Believe me, they don't put this much cloth into clothing nowadays."

Nelly's face fell at sound of the price and she swallowed. "I don't have that much money," she said.

"It's worth twice what I'm asking," said the woman, "but since you're my first customer today, I'll let it go for twenty francs." She reverently lowered her voice. "This gown has danced in a king's palace," she announced.

Then the Monkey Man roared, "We offer eight francs —and it's worth twice that to have someone carry the old rag away."

Nelly was shocked at his disrespect for a gown that had danced in a royal palace and which still had the chance to dance in a carnival.

"I have eleven francs," she said.

"Then I'll let you have it for that because I like you," said the woman.

F. R.

But the Monkey Man caught Nelly's hand as she reached for her francs. "Would you rob a child?" he demanded fiercely of the woman. "Eleven francs for an old rag that somebody threw into the ash can?"

The woman began to whine. "My prices are so low that I'm not even making a living," she declared. "I'm getting poorer and poorer every day. Soon I will be penniless, then I will have to give up this stall."

The Monkey Man snorted. "Your prices are so high that your customers are getting poorer and poorer," he accused. "You are a robber, madame. Forgive me for saying so, but you are a robber, a thief, and an embezzler. I shall call the police. Justice shall be done." He looked over his shoulder as if searching for a policeman in the crowd. Nelly was terrified. She did not want the woman arrested, especially if she was so poor.

"I don't really want the gown," she gulped. "I don't think it would look good on my mother."

But as she stepped back, the woman reached over the counter and grabbed her shoulder. "Eleven francs if it is for your dear mother," she wheedled.

Nelly wanted the dress at that price, but she didn't wish to gain it by a falsehood. "It isn't really for my mother," she confessed. "It's for a goose."

"Pah!" exclaimed the woman. "Only a goose would

wear such a freakish old creation. Eight francs and it's yours."

Nelly counted out the money while the woman folded the dress and wrapped it in a newspaper. "Good, durable cloth," she said with a change of heart, "and when it wears out, you'll still have the beads."

Nelly carried the bundle tightly in her arms. This treasure was now hers—Arabelle's—and she still had some money left over.

As they left the Flea Market they saw a man selling peanuts. He wore a woman's big hat trimmed with strings of peanuts to attract customers. To show her appreciation to the Monkey Man for his kindness and help, Nelly bought a sack of nuts for his monkeys.

Then the Monkey Man bought three sacks for her and himself and Marc. "I might as well spend my money on peanuts," he said. "After seeing the saws they're selling in there, I think my own is in first-class condition."

CHAPTER EIGHT

The Petit Cirque Flandin

There were exclamations of delight from all the Flandins when they saw the good bargain Nelly had made at the Flea Market.

"My mother wore such a gown when she sold tickets for the merry-go-round," said Mama with a mist of remembrance in her eyes.

"It's not too bad," said Uncle Bruno. "Sort of grabs your eyes."

"I'll help you make the costume for Arabelle," offered Odile, but she politely declined when her little sister offered her the waist for a blouse. "It is much too old for me," she said, "and the sleeves would split when I work the goats on the stage."

87

Nelly made sure that the kids were busy playing elsewhere before they laid the purple gown on the outdoor table and opened Mama's sewing basket. Odile cut one long piece after another from the skirt and sewed them together, then gathered them into a smaller but fuller ruffled skirt for Arabelle's plump figure. The goose looked more like a great purple ostrich, with scarlet roses for wing tips.

As they cut and sewed, Odile and Nelly thought of other things to create from the cuttings. A round piece of cloth with the green beads on it gathered into an adorable bonnet, and a scarlet rose gave it a coquettish air.

"When I have time," said Nelly, "I can take off some of the beads and string them into a necklace for Arabelle."

Odile looked at Arabelle's long neck. "For the present, we will make her a scarf," she said.

She cut an extra long ribbon and wrapped it around and around the goose's long neck.

"She looks like a chorus girl with a sore throat," said Fernand, "but hurry, hurry! The first show starts at three o'clock and Marc has already moved the animals out front to collect a crowd. Perhaps Arabelle can open the free show."

Nelly objected even as Marc had. "She's too good to

be free," she said. But even so, she agreed to let the people have a free look at Arabelle in her original creation which might have come from a salon of high fashion. She led her to the midway and joined the curious crowd in front of the Petit Cirque Flandin.

The midway was full of people for the opening afternoon, and the air was full of noise. Music from dozens of merry-go-rounds blended into a lively medley which could not drown the shouts of hundreds of barkers. There

was the bang, bang, bang of rifles at the shooting galleries and the muffled roar of the roller coaster. Hawkers cried their goods and motors rumbled. And over all hovered the tantalizing smell of fried food and baked gingerbread.

Nelly looked proudly at the picture on front of the circus. She thought that it didn't need a great arena and seals to make it good. It was the best circus in the world.

People strolled by, laughed, and pointed at Arabelle in her finery of yesterday. "Regard my great-aunt Sabine," laughed one woman.

Many of them stopped to look at the other animals too. The three dogs, chained on a high platform, were growling and quarreling among themselves because Marc had put them in the wrong places. Dodo belonged in the middle. The goats were placidly staring back at the people and waggling their goatees. Nanette's kids chased each other up steps, over barricades, and finally climbed to the highest platform with the dogs.

Odile led the two ponies out and tied them near the entrance. Then Fernand brought the fancy yellow pompoms and fastened them in place between their ears. The ponies proudly tossed their heads and snorted.

Nelly was so proud of them it almost gave her a fever.

No, no, those clever animals could never live in the farm-yard of a quiet village.

Fernand began the free show. His nose was painted red and his hair combed forward. He told funny jokes all the time he was juggling some balls. It gave Nelly a pang to see that the people were more interested in the animals than Fernand's quips.

But when Marc did his somersaults everyone forgot the animals. Because after he had turned ten, he somer-saulted right off the platform to the ground. Those in front rushed to help him to his feet and see that he hadn't broken any bones. Then more curiosity seekers gathered around and Marc really attracted a bigger crowd than if he had performed all his somersaults successfully.

"Tickets!" bawled Papa. "Buy your tickets for the gigantic spectacle which is about to begin inside!"

To Nelly's bewilderment, most of the big crowd quickly walked away. Only a few stood in line for tickets.

Odile hurried to the entrance and took their tickets. She held out her hand to each one for a tip because any money she made this way was her own.

The old phonograph began grinding out a lively march. Mama beckoned to Nelly. "Have Arabelle dance," she implored. "That may bring more customers."

Nelly was disappointed that she wouldn't get to see the opening acts herself but she was more disappointed at the small number who had bought tickets. She led Arabelle up on the platform. Like a bandleader she waved her arm back and forth. Arabelle danced a bit clumsily in her finery. A few more people bought tickets.

Marc burst out of the circus with his eyes shining. "I did all my twenty-four somersaults and didn't fall off the stage," he cried. His face fell. "But only three people clapped for me. It's your turn now—I mean Arabelle's. Soon as Uncle Bruno brings the goats out front and makes room inside."

Keeping the animals in front when they weren't performing served two purposes: it attracted customers and it kept the performers within easy reach when it was their turn inside.

Out came the goats and in went Nelly followed by Arabelle. The audience on the wooden benches clapped politely. Nelly was vexed to see that it was much smaller than the one that had gathered at the market of St. Germain-en-Laye to watch the goose.

Arabelle marched to the center of the stage and thrust out her neck in a hostile gesture as if to say, "Anyone who isn't going to like my act better leave right now."

She went through her dance in a slow, disinterested

way, much to Nelly's impatience. Then the goose stopped dancing completely and sat down in the middle of the stage with a bored air. No matter how frantically Nelly waved her arms, Arabelle acted as if she did not see her. She seemed to have something else on her mind.

Arabelle refused to budge. The audience fidgeted and Nelly heard a little boy say to his mother, "But when is that duck going to *do* something?"

Then Arabelle rose to her yellow feet with great dignity and gave her purple ruffles a shrug. Disdainfully she waddled off the stage, but, wonder of wonders, where she had sat was a big white egg. Arabelle had laid her first egg.

How the audience clapped and cheered! And Nelly heard one lady remark to another, "Such a clever little girl to teach a goose to lay an egg like that."

"I will have to bring my grandchildren tomorrow afternoon to see the goose lay her egg," replied the other.

Marc passed a basket among the people so they could drop in tips for the animals. They gave generously because they thought the well-trained goose deserved a tip.

Nelly was thrilled but frightened by Arabelle's unrehearsed act. What would the lady say if her grandchildren were disappointed next afternoon? How could she ever get Arabelle to lay an egg at every performance, especially as there would be four a day?

Of course Arabelle laid no more eggs at the other performances that day, although she danced with a free mind and more spirit. But something happened to save Nelly the embarrassment of failure before the lady's grandchildren.

That evening as they were eating the cheese omelet that Mama had made from Arabelle's wonderful egg, Papa announced, "There will be no performance tomorrow afternoon."

"No performance tomorrow afternoon!" exclaimed Odile. "Why?"

"No performance on Easter afternoon!" roared Uncle

Bruno. "The biggest day of the Fair!"

Papa shook his head. "There will be no performance tomorrow afternoon because it *is* Easter," he said. "For ten years we have worked without any rest or holiday. This Easter afternoon we are going to have our holiday —all of us together as a family."

"But the money we will lose," cried Fernand. "We are only making both ends meet. And we owe Uncle Simon and Aunt Barbe."

"We can't afford a holiday," said Uncle Bruno. "You may be sure the animals aren't going to take any holiday from eating."

"If we wait until we are rich," said Papa, "we will never have a holiday. Besides, we are going to have a useful holiday."

"How can any carnival worker's holiday be useful?" asked Uncle Bruno.

"We are all going to see a performance at the famous Cirque de Paris," said Papa. "You remember our old friend Dany the juggler is with them now. It will do us good to see a big circus like that. We might learn a few new tricks."

"We will learn how much a big circus like that charges for its tickets," put in Mama. "That is what we will learn."

95

"Perhaps we don't charge enough," said Uncle Bruno. "One franc to see such well-trained animals as ours is charity."

"And we'll be on charity if we spend our francs to see a fine, fancy circus," complained Mama. "We don't make too many of them."

"And we should do best on Easter," said Odile, "the biggest day of our circus. I was planning to buy a new blouse if I make enough money in tips tomorrow."

But Nelly was trembling with excitement at the idea of having an outing with her family—as real families did. She was fearful that the others might talk Papa out of their holiday. But they couldn't. No matter what they said, they couldn't change Papa's mind because he had already bought the tickets. Perhaps he had bought them early and secretly for that very reason.

He held up the pieces of paper triumphantly, and that ended the arguments immediately. They certainly weren't going to feed their tickets to the goats.

The Cirque de Paris! They began talking about it as excitedly as if they had all clamored to go.

"The Rinaldo brothers run it," said Papa, "and they are famous throughout Europe."

Mama sighed. "A permanent circus in a well-built theater," she dreamed. "What a change for Dany! Settled in Paris with his family during the cold months like a regular baker or clerk. He doesn't have to take to the roads until summer, and then the whole family travels together."

"I wish we could get a contract with the Cirque de Paris," said Fernand, "but rich chance that the Rinaldos would ever come to the Gingerbread Fair scouting for acts. Sooner the kings will come down from their monuments and stand in line for tickets."

Nelly began to tremble again. If only the Flandins could work at the famous Cirque. There would be no more money worries, the animals would be safe from the fate which had overtaken the farmer's pigs, and best of all, the Flandins would have a real home life. She and Marc could go to school in Paris.

"If only those Rinaldos could see Arabelle," she cried. "I bet they don't have a goose that dances in their circus, no matter how good it is."

"I'm sure they would want the goat act if they saw it," said Odile. "Noisette and Nanette get better every performance. Sometimes they go all the way through a trick without making a mistake. And I have some ideas for using the kids."

Marc was carried away by their dreams. "If I practice more I think I'll be able to turn fifty somersaults in succession," he said. "Do you suppose those Rinaldos have anyone who can do that, Papa?"

"Right now I don't know what the Rinaldos have beside Dany," said Papa, "but we'll all know by this time tomorrow. And all isn't lost because we'll still catch the Easter evening crowds. We'll have to," he added grimly, "because I spent all the grocery money on those tickets."

Mama let out a shrill cry at this. "Our food money! And pray what will we eat if no one comes to our show tomorrow night?"

"Hay and raw sugar beets and dog food," said Uncle Bruno. "We still have a fair supply of them, because the animals have always come first."

"Perhaps Arabelle will lay another egg," said Nelly timidly. She realized that Aunt Barbe's remark about a time for a goose to lay eggs had some sense to it. "Besides," she remembered, "I still have two francs."

CHAPTER NINE

The Cirque de Paris

Nelly could not understand why Arabelle's act did not
draw a bigger audience. Even when the goose danced in
the free show outside, the crowds still melted away when
the performance was over.

That evening she and Marc were given permission to
wander around on the midway and see the sights of the
carnival. The whole street from the Place du Nation to
the Porte de Vincennes was a fairyland of light and
music. The crowd was greater than during the afternoon.

The children watched a group of army aviators line
up to buy tickets for the toy airplanes that swung over
the heads of the crowd. They yearned to ride in the
airplanes themselves but did not want to use Nelly's two

francs because Mama might need them to buy food.

They stood in front of a shooting gallery where men fired rifles at the moving figures of cardboard bears. If a target was hit, a hidden machine made a ferocious growl.

They watched the free show of the fire-eating men from Africa, but when the natives had finished their dance and had gone inside, the little Flandins had to

wander on. They did so want to see the giant hidden behind curtains. The barker was holding up his enormous shoe to lure the audience inside.

But they could afford to see the great light and water display in the middle of the street because it was free for everyone.

Regretfully they had to return home after that.

"And we still haven't found the Candy Man," Nelly reminded her brother.

"What do we care about Papa's beard or gingerbread pigs?" asked Marc. "We are going to a real circus tomorrow."

And truthfully Nelly didn't mind leaving the carnival on the afternoon of Easter because that was an even greater adventure.

"We will go by the Métro," said Papa. "It is cheaper and faster."

The underground Métro station wasn't far from their trailer house. First they made sure that the animals would be all right. Nelly and Marc hauled more pails of water so they would not go thirsty. The goats and ponies were put back in the truck with dependable Dodo, and the other dogs shut up in the trailer. The Monkey Man offered to take Arabelle because his little racers were so interested in her.

At last everything had been arranged, and the family proudly walked down the steps that led into the station. The Métro was an underground railway with all its stations and tracks in the basement of Paris. Getting there was not so fast as Papa had said. They had to ask which train to take and were lost for a time in long tiled tunnels through which rushed people who knew exactly what trains they wanted.

The Flandins went through a gate and stepped out on a long, lighted platform with big signs that said PORTE DE VINCENNES. A roar came from the dark tunnel and a great dragon of a train slid toward them. It had many gray cars and a few red ones. The Flandins were pushed into a gray car by the people in back of them.

"We must keep together," warned Papa. "The ticket woman said we change at the first stop."

They kept together as best they could although the other passengers squeezed them, and a fat man fell into Odile's lap when they went around a dark curve. The dragon train roared on through tunnels which led to another station platform.

"Reuilly-Diderot," shouted Fernand, pointing to a sign on the station where they were stopping. The Flandins battled their way through the crowd to get off.

They had to walk through more tiled tunnels and swinging steel arms.

Their new train was made up of green and red cars. The family stepped into a red one because it stopped nearest them. All the seats were taken so they had to stand.

At Bastille, a man in a blue uniform got on. "Tickets, tickets," he bawled, weaving his way through the passengers.

Papa pulled the tickets from his pocket although they had already been punched. The man glared at them.

"Aha!" he gloated. "Sneaking into first-class on second-class tickets."

Papa did not understand him. "What do you mean first-class and second-class?" he asked.

"Don't try to fool me," shouted the Métro man. "You know as well as I that the red cars are first-class. There will be a fine of two francs apiece. Seven tickets. That is fourteen francs."

"Fourteen francs," gasped Mama. "A taxi would have been cheaper."

"We don't even have seats," exploded Uncle Bruno. "This is what I call traveling fourth-class."

But no amount of arguing could change the man's

mind or heart. Papa opened his worn purse and counted out his last coins. Nelly offered her two francs. Even with that Fernand had to put in two postage stamps to make the sum.

"I warn you," thundered Uncle Bruno, shaking his knobby fist under the Métro man's big nose. "We are going to hire the best lawyer in Paris and fight this thing through all the courts."

The other shrugged. "It won't be my worry," he said. "I don't own the Métro."

"We will have to walk home," Papa told the family. "It will give us an appetite."

"An appetite for what?" demanded Mama. "Hay and dog food? There is no money for groceries."

"Watch for Filles du Calvaire," said Papa to change the subject. "That is where we get off."

"And if we don't get off there," said Uncle Bruno, "Heaven knows what will happen to us. We'll spend the rest of our lives lost in tunnels like trapped miners."

Nelly shivered at the very thought. What would happen to Arabelle and all the animals if the Flandins never came out of the Métro?

Her worries were in vain because everyone got out of the car at the next stop. They went up steps, and to their surprise they found themselves on the pretty Place Pasdeloup with its monument and plane trees.

"Well, we made it," said Papa proudly.

"Look!" cried Nelly. "The Cirque de Paris!"

All eyes turned to the circular building topped by a cupola and decorated with a border of horse scenes. Guarding the entrance were statues of horses carrying Roman riders.

The Flandins rushed across the fan-shaped patterns of the cobblestones. They stared at the giant posters on the cream-colored wall. One showed a beautiful girl with a golden crown standing on a white horse's back while white doves swirled around her. "Queen of the Circus World," announced the poster.

"It will probably be some girl on an old plug with a pair of tame pigeons," predicted Uncle Bruno.

But Odile looked longingly at the girl's picture. How unimportant to be Esmeralda of a carnival when that lucky girl had been elected queen of the whole circus world.

"I'd surely like to get a contract with this outfit," said Papa. "They've got a fine building."

"And they don't have to take it down and put it up again every few weeks," said Uncle Bruno.

"Their performers can stay in Paris for the winter," sighed Mama. "They can have their children with them all the time."

Nelly's heart beat faster. "Why can't we work here, Papa?" she asked. "Why wouldn't the owners want our acts—especially Arabelle?"

"Because they've never seen or heard of us," answered Odile. "It's hard to get a big circus interested in people like us."

"It's their loss," said Fernand airily. "They don't know what they're missing."

"They don't even know that the best somersaulter in the world is standing right in front of their building," boasted Marc.

"I bet they don't have a goat act," said Odile.

Nelly felt humiliated. To think that some of the best circus performers in Europe had to enter the Cirque de Paris like any common audience!

In the red and gold foyer they saw a huge picture of the circus owners. One of them had black hair and a black mustache which couldn't completely cover his friendly mouth. "Arturo Rinaldo," was written under his picture, "manager of the colossal Cirque de Paris."

The circus theater was bright red and the ring was covered with a great circle of canvas. The seats ran in tiers all the way up the sides, and the roof was shaped like the top of an ornate tent. Over the entranceways reared lifelike figures of horses. If only the Flandins could perform in such a grand place! Imagine Arabelle dancing in that big ring. Best of all, imagine the Flandins together through the whole winter. That is just what Nelly was imagining when she looked up the steep steps of the aisle to see a man with a familiar face talking to an usher. First she thought the man in the top hat and long tails was someone she knew well. Then she remembered. It was his picture they had seen in the foyer. He was the Rinaldo who managed the Cirque de Paris.

Nelly felt cold, then she felt hot. The sudden idea in her head made her dizzy. She stood up and hesitantly bit her thumb for a moment. Then she darted up the steps before anyone noticed she had left. Straight to Mr. Rinaldo she went. She was frightened by her own nerve, but she managed to tug the long-tailed coat. The owner turned to look down at her with annoyance.

"Oh, Monsieur Rinaldo," she cried. "I'm Nelly Flandin. I'm a goose. I mean I've got a goose. A real goose. We all have geese. I mean we all have animals."

The man smiled at Nelly's agitation. He stooped over and braced her shoulders with his hands. "Now relax, little one," he said. "I can see that you are not a goose. You are a frightened little girl because you're lost and can't find your parents."

"No, no," cried Nelly, pointing down the tiers of seats. "There's my family."

And they were where she pointed, all their heads turned around and all their mouths open.

"We have a carnival circus," she went on, "but we want to work here for you. We have trained animal acts and I have a wonderful goose that dances. And we've done it all with kindness and patience because we love our animals. You can ask Dany the juggler. He knows us."

Her eyes were so pleading that Arturo Rinaldo patted her head in a friendly manner even though he had to say, "I'm sorry, but all our acts are booked for the season, little girl."

He shook her hand in farewell and Nelly clung to his tightly. "If you'd only come to see our circus—the Petit

Cirque Flandin at the Gingerbread Fair," she begged, "I know you would want us to work for you." As he stepped away, she said reproachfully, "Since we've come to see your circus, it's only fair that you should visit ours."

He flashed a last polite but impatient smile at her, then disappeared with the usher.

Slowly Nelly stepped down to her seat.

"What were you doing?" demanded Mama.

"What were you saying to that man?" asked Fernand.

"Don't you know that was one of the Rinaldo brothers?" asked Papa.

"Yes, I know," said Nelly, "and he knows who we are now."

The band suddenly broke into a loud, lively march. The canvas cover was rolled away from the sawdust ring. The house lights were dimmed and the show began. Such a show as the Flandins had never expected to see anywhere on earth.

A whole cavalry of horses came galloping in. They had numbers on their sides and slowly they jockeyed into place until they made a line running correctly from one to twenty.

"They can count," gasped Nelly.

"It isn't the number they know," said Papa. "Each one

is used to running behind a certain horse so that is why they find their places so easily."

That wasn't all the horses could do. Each one mounted a great drum and slowly turned around and around in perfect time.

"Perhaps I could teach the ponies to do that," said Papa.

The horses formed a ring, walked on their hind legs, and finally bowed to the audience with shoulders down and one foreleg thrust gracefully forward in the same perfect time. Then they fell into line again and all but one cantered out of the ring. The remaining horse neighed in time to the music. Then it stamped out answers to questions asked by its trainer and worked simple arithmetic problems in that way.

Papa had no more to say about the ponies. Each Flandin knew well that the ponies could never be trained to do anything so remarkable—not by any one of them.

"I didn't even know the answers to some of those questions myself," admitted Marc.

"And I can't add and subtract in my head like that," said Nelly. "Such a smart horse."

"It isn't the horse that's so smart," said Uncle Bruno. "It's the trainer. He has taught the horse to stamp a certain number of times. Has some hidden signals the horse understands. Perhaps he rubs his shoe against the floor or clicks a feather in his pocket."

Clowns came on next, and such funny ones the Flandins had never seen. One was dressed like a tramp, with a huge nose, an old derby, and frogman flippers for shoes. But the most unusual one was wearing a gorgeous knee-length coat covered with flashing sequins and glittering beads—like a coat of lights. It sparkled and gleamed in the spotlights and the clown seemed an oriental prince even though his face was painted white, his ears red, and he had only one big black eyebrow shaped like a question mark.

"Perhaps I should make my ears red instead of my nose," said Fernand, "and that eyebrow make-up is pretty slick." But he didn't say anything about the jeweled coat.

There were other acts, bigger and better than anything the Flandins had expected. Even Dany had improved since his carnival days.

The most spectacular act of all was the finale. The Flandins immediately recognized the Queen of the Circus World as she rode into the ring standing on the back of a great white horse. She was dressed in red velvet, as the poster showed, with the golden crown on her head. It stayed on, too, even when she turned somersaults on the horse.

Nelly stole a quick sideways look at Odile. Her sister was slumped in her seat with her chin wedged between her fists. She had been very silent all through the show.

Suddenly a fluttering of hundreds of wings made the audience start and gasp. Nelly even screamed. Hundreds of white doves came swooping from cages hidden in the roof. They flew in a cloud, circling lower and lower. Some of them perched on the horse's head and mane, others on its flanks. Some settled on the queen's crown and shoulders, and one lone bird suspended itself before her face, like a hummingbird about to sip a flower, and pecked at her lips.

The audience burst into wild applause. The poster didn't show the circus the way the Rinaldos wished it might look. It showed it the way it actually was.

Lights went on. The audience began rushing along the passages and scrambling down the steps like frightened ants. The Flandins were pushed along with them.

CHAPTER TEN

Esmeralda

Outside, the Flandins all turned to have one last look at the Cirque de Paris, for each knew in his heart that he would never see it again.

The big city circus which should have made them so happy had only filled them with shame and disappointment. They trudged down the street on the long walk back to the Gingerbread Fair.

"No wonder we can't make any money with our circus," said Papa. "It isn't any good."

"We have a grubby, scrubby, flea-bitten circus," declared Fernand.

"It's a crusty little circus full of crumby little acts," said Marc. "Mine, too."

Uncle Bruno tried to console them. "What do they expect to see for one franc?" he asked.

Papa started to walk more briskly and raised his shoulders. "For one franc they should see the best show we can give," he said with dignity.

Then all the Flandins held their heads higher because they knew they had always done their best. And if a trick hadn't gone off right the first time, they had kept trying until it succeeded. They couldn't stay discouraged long because they were carnival people and used to making the best of things.

"We'll make the circus better," announced Papa.

"I will paint a picture of a polar bear on a trapeze in front," added Uncle Bruno, because he thought that was the easiest and quickest way to improve the Petit Cirque Flandin.

But Nelly knew they were only trying to be brave. Since she had seen the graceful doves swooping through the air and perching on the horse and rider, she realized that Arabelle's dance wasn't marvelous at all. Any old farm goose could flap her wings and dance around. Then a sudden fright gripped her. Suppose Arturo Rinaldo did come to see their circus! How ashamed they would be. She hoped with all her might that the circus manager would forget all about the little girl who had so brazenly bragged about her trained goose.

It was Mama who had the unhappiest thought of all. She had just noticed a clock over a store. "We won't have time to put on any more shows tonight. It's so late and we still have a long way to go. We'll be too tired. And the animals must be fed. We can't expect them to work on empty stomachs."

"It will be our stomachs that are empty," said Uncle Bruno.

"We've spent all our money," added Odile. "What will we eat tomorrow?"

"We always have plenty of goat's milk and there's still some of the cheese," said Mama cheerfully. "There's nothing like homemade country cheese."

"I'm sick of cheese," whined Marc. "I never did like cheese, even on the farm."

"All the more for the rest of us," said Fernand. "You can eat lobster and pressed duck and new spring asparagus."

Strangely enough it was Uncle Bruno who knew what to do. "People are always feeding the animals when they are out in front," he said. "I'll put a big basket on the platfrom with a sign over it saying 'Please leave food for our animals here.' Then we'll eat it ourselves."

"That sounds like begging," said Papa.

"How about 'We accept food for our animals'?" asked Mama. "That sounds more as if we are doing them a favor."

"I think it should be 'We accept cakes and candy for our animals—but not cheese,'" said Marc.

No one paid any attention to him.

"We'll give the animals half to make it fair," said Mama.

"And they better start improving their performances," said Uncle Bruno darkly. "They're the ones who should have seen the Cirque de Paris, not us."

"We must all improve," said Papa. "We must have more kindness and patience."

Nelly was not encouraged. After all the kindness and patience she had spent on Arabelle, all the goose had learned was something any goose already knew.

But when they arrived at their carnival home, the Monkey Man had news that gave her new hope.

"You should have seen my monkey Myro and Arabelle dancing together!" he exclaimed. "Believe me you don't have to go to the Cirque de Paris to see a great act. Just like a ballet pair they were, with Myro aping every step of the goose."

Nelly was happy again. Arabelle was still a star. "Can they perform together sometime?" she cried, clapping her hands.

"It would take a long time to train them," said the Monkey Man. "I kept Myro on his chain all the time and didn't let him get too close to Arabelle. You never can tell what a monkey will do. If only we could trust him loose, what an act that would be!"

Nelly could already see it in her mind—Arabelle dancing so gracefully in her costume, with Myro in his little uniform, bowing and waltzing with one paw lightly around Arabelle's neck and the other fluttering through

the air. And there in the front row was Monsieur Rinaldo clapping madly.

Papa looked at all their faces as they sat around the table under the street light eating the last of the cheese and some leftovers Mama had warmed.

"Cheer up!" he urged. "The Gingerbread Fair has just begun and it has a whole month to run. We may get rich yet."

Mama smiled. "Remember the old proverb," she said. " 'Tomorrow is a little gift of hope.' "

The little gift of hope was enough to fill the hearts of seven people who had felt so depressed only a little while before.

They didn't starve either. Unknown friends of their animals dropped crusts of bread, pieces of sausage, scraps of lettuce, and even a gingerbread pig that had been baptized "Henri" into the basket under the new sign.

Mama made bread pudding and a casserole with some of the scraps. She invented a soup of her own from goat's milk and meat tidbits which Papa named Poor Jean's Broth just as if it were on the menu of the fancy café where the Fair committee was meeting. It was having a dinner to decide which lucky girl should be the Esmeralda of that year's carnival.

The Flandins were eating Poor Jean's Broth at the table between shows when the roller-coaster owner, who was chairman of the committee, stopped by. He took off his cap and bowed deeply to Odile.

"My compliments, mademoiselle," he said in a courtly manner. "You have been elected Esmeralda of this year's Gingerbread Fair."

The Flandins were overjoyed. They invited the man to share their unusual soup, but he told them he was full of beefsteak and oysters and *pâté de fois gras*. Odile was so happy she couldn't eat any more herself. She led Nanette from under the circus floor, took off her shoes, and did a little barefoot dance under the chestnuts while the white goat pranced around her.

"Perhaps I can use that purple beaded waist after all," she told Nelly. "It will look so Gypsyish. And I'll borrow the fortuneteller's big earrings. And you and Marc can be my boy and girl of honor."

"When is the coronation?" asked Mama.

"Day after tomorrow," said Odile, "out on the midway in the afternoon."

"That's fine," said Mama. "The children won't be going back to the farm until the next day."

Nelly and Marc turned unhappy faces to her.

"You mean we have to go back?" asked Nelly with

tears welling up in her eyes.

"You know that is the way it was planned," answered Mama. "You were to spend Easter vacation with us."

But that wasn't the way Nelly and Marc had planned it at all. Everything had turned out wrong for them.

"If only Monsieur Rinaldo would come to our show," Nelly confided to the Monkey Man later, "perhaps everything would go off better than usual and he would want us after all. He doesn't have any goats or geese."

The Monkey Man sympathized with her, but he couldn't offer much hope.

"If the Cirque de Paris doesn't have any goats or geese, it's because they don't want them," he told her. "They can have their pick of the best acts in all of Europe, so you really can't expect them to come looking for a bargain at a carnival."

Nelly and Marc wandered disconsolately through the noisy lighted midway that night. Their acts weren't attracting any larger crowds and they had lost all hope of joining the Cirque de Paris.

Not even finding the Candy Man could make them any happier. He had set up his little stand near the merry-go-rounds and was making the fluffy candy right in sight of his waiting customers. He had a big tin drum with a blower and blue flame in the center. From two little bowls filled with pink and blue sugar crystals, he dropped one spoonful after another into the drum. The flames melted the sugar and the blower spun it into rainbow-tinted cotton which he expertly swirled around long sticks.

Remembering his promise, he gathered extra large clouds onto two sticks, one in each hand, and gave them to Nelly and Marc.

Nelly hated to tell him the news about the election of Esmeralda, even though she was so proud of her sister. "I wish there could be two of them," she ended.

But the man did not seem to mind. "My Marie won't be disappointed," he informed her. "She is getting married at St. Gabriel's Church down the street Wednesday morning so she'll have her chance to get dressed up and have a crowd stare at her. And I'm doing even better business here than I did at the Fair of St. Michael in Le Havre."

So the family of Esmeralda might have envied him instead.

"You must come and see my goose dance," Nelly invited him. "We'll let you in free." She swallowed. "You better come soon though, because we'll be leaving."

123

They went all the way to the false abbey and found the false monks giving away little cubes of their gingerbread.

"Fill your pockets," said the false monk whose brown habit had fooled Nelly the first day. "We're paid to get rid of it."

They didn't have to be invited twice. They decided to take the samples of spiced bread home for the family, and Nelly planned to save a few pieces for Arabelle.

CHAPTER ELEVEN

Arabelle and Myro

Nelly and Marc carried the pails of water silently. They didn't seem any heavier than their own hearts.

"One good thing is that we'll have only a couple more days to do this," Marc began speaking in an unconcerned way.

"We will be doing the farm chores," Nelly reminded him. "We'll be grinding sugar beets for poor old Forte and feeding those silly quacking ducks."

"And that old black and white cow," said Marc, changing his mood. "She'll have to be milked every morning and night." Neither could find the courage to say, "And we'll be far away from the family."

Nelly lingered around the animals after they had

been watered. She patted Guy's thick mane and Grisette's fat gray back. Strange that the thinner the family became, the fatter the ponies grew. Guy pushed his wet little nose into her pocket, so Nelly gave him a stale piece of gingerbread which she had been saving. Then she threw her arms around his shaggy mane. What would happen to the darling ponies if some miracle didn't save the Petit Cirque Flandin?

The kids were jealous of Nelly's attention to the ponies. One of them butted Guy's hind leg. But the other was more clever. He began to nibble on Nelly's sweater, because he knew that nothing would get attention sooner.

Nelly jumped back and pushed him away with a laugh. Then she pulled him close and gave him a big hug too. She didn't dare think of what might happen to tender little goats whose circus couldn't support them any longer.

Of course Dodo wanted attention too because after all he was the dog star. He walked on his hind legs and did some quick turns for her. Nelly clapped and fondled him in turn. Faithful little Dodo. Anyone would be lucky to have such a good watchdog, but not many farmers would be able to appreciate his tricks.

She wiped her eyes on the cuff of her sweater, unfastened Guy's halter, and led him out front. It was almost time for the first afternoon performance. She would bring the kids out too, but she would have to watch them to see that they didn't eat anyone's clothing.

Uncle Bruno helped line up the animals on their platforms. Mama went into the ticket cage and began rummaging around helplessly. "I don't know what I'll use for change if the customers need it," she sighed.

But no one heard her. Marc had begun his somersaulting, and Fernand was busy somewhere putting on his make-up.

The usual crowd began to gather. They clapped politely for Marc, but they were more interested in watching the kids chase each other from platform to platform.

Nelly began thinking that she better find Arabelle and dress her in her costume. There wouldn't be many more performances for the goose. Soon she would be going back to the farm to waddle around with the ducks and lay eggs for Aunt Barbe.

As Nelly turned, she bumped into a brown suit. "Please excuse me, monsieur," she said to its owner as she raised her eyes to his face. Then she stood staring at him with goggling eyes and gaping mouth. It was Arturo Rinaldo! He had come to see the Petit Cirque Flandin.

"If it isn't the little goose girl!" he exclaimed. "You

127

see I have accepted your kind invitation."

Nelly's first thought was to fly to her family and warn them that they must do their best because Arturo Rinaldo would be in the audience. But she couldn't run off rudely and leave him.

He pointed to the pictures over the front of the building. "Is it really that big inside?" he asked with a twinkle in his eyes.

Nelly had to be truthful. "Oh, no, monsieur," she answered. "It isn't big at all. We don't have any seals or cats and only two horses. And they're really ponies."

Monsieur Rinaldo pointed to the sign that read, "We train our animals with kindness and patience."

"I suppose that isn't true either," he said.

Nelly flared up. "Indeed it is," she stoutly maintained. "Our animals are just like part of our family. Papa won't let anyone use a whip. And I trained my goose with kindness and patience." She remembered old Forte. "I did kick a farm horse once because he frightened Arabelle, but I'm sorry."

Over and over rolled Marc in his somersaults. If only she could catch his eye. He was doing them so half-heartedly because he thought he would soon be returning to the farm.

128

"I'll get your ticket," offered Nelly. "It will be free for you."

She pushed her way through the crowd and sprang up the steps to the ticket cage. "Monsieur Rinaldo," she whispered loudly through the wicket to her mother. "Monsieur Arturo Rinaldo is down there. He's coming to our show. Tell everybody, and give me a free ticket for him."

Uncle Bruno, standing near the entrance, heard her. "He should pay for it," he grumbled. "We paid to go to his circus—and it cost plenty."

But Mama nervously tore off a ticket and pressed it into Nelly's moist hand.

Nelly ran down to find her guest. As she came up behind him, she saw a horrifying sight. One of the kids whom she was supposed to be watching was nibbling on his handsome brown jacket. It had already nibbled a fringed hole.

Nelly jerked the kid away. She frantically apologized to the circus owner. She gathered the kid into her arms.

"Oh, perhaps I should punish him, monsieur," she admitted, "but I can't. He's so cute and he doesn't know any better."

Monsieur Rinaldo ruefully picked at the cut threads

but he did not demand a new jacket. Nelly gave him the crushed ticket. "If you will excuse me," she said, "I must go and get my goose. She's with the Monkey Man."

First she securely locked the kids in the truck. Then her feet flew over the pavement and hopped across the power cables as she raced to the Monkey Man's little speedway. Already the monkeys were chained on their platform and were collecting their own crowd. They

F.R.

were peering, gesticulating, and chattering together because they thought the people had such funny faces and did such funny things.

Nelly raced up the steps and inside the doorway where she knew the Monkey Man would be testing his electric cars with Arabelle waddling around his feet.

"Oh, monsieur," she shrieked, "he's at our circus! He really came after all!"

"Who is *he?*" asked the Monkey Man. "King Philippe Auguste or St. Anthony or the President of the Republic?"

"Arturo Rinaldo who manages the Cirque de Paris," cried Nelly.

"That's even more extraordinary," said the Monkey Man.

"Honk, honk," said Arabelle, with great surprise in her honks.

Nelly twisted her hands together beseechingly. "Please, monsieur," she begged, "may Myro dance with Arabelle? It would be such a fine act for Monsieur Rinaldo to see—so different."

The Monkey Man spun the driving wheel of a little car. "There's no telling how it would turn out," he said. "Monkeys are mischievous. Myro might dance as neatly as a monkey on a stick. Then again he might take it into his head to pull out Arabelle's tail feathers or climb up on the roof."

Nelly was frantic. "We've got to take the chance," she explained. "It's my only chance. You know any goose can flap its wings and dance, and so does Monsieur Rinaldo."

"But not with a monkey for a partner," agreed the man. "I'd like to see how that act would turn out myself. I'll hold my show off until later and come over with Myro. I must stand somewhere out of sight to watch him in case anything goes wrong."

Nelly informed Uncle Bruno about the new act as it was his business to announce it.

When Nelly and the Monkey Man crept to the back of the stage and peeped in, Odile had finished with Noisette and was putting Nanette through her stunts. Gracefully, as Esmeralda, she danced around Nanette and coaxed her up on the narrow plank. But the goat was not in the mood for showing off. Halfway across she refused to go any farther. She looked right at Arturo Rinaldo on his hard bench and said "ba-a-a" scornfully.

Odile tried to get her to kneel on the plank by lightly tapping her front legs with the crop, but Nanette only waggled her goatee. Odile was so busy that she often turned her back to the audience, showing the telltale iron burn on her blouse.

She directed the goat to jump up on the large ball. Nanette saucily jumped over it instead. Any other trainer might have been so out of patience as to bring the riding crop down on Nanette's head with a heavy crack, but Odile kept speaking softly to her. At last she had to give up. She curtsied to the audience and said, "I hope you will forgive my goat, but she is a mother and it is past her kids' mealtime."

Uncle Bruno, in his long, uneven coattails, glared at Nanette as she trotted off the stage. "And now, *mesdames et messieurs*," he said, changing his scowl to a smile, "we present the great troupe of trained Flandin dogs in some of the most remarkable feats ever executed by canines."

He hurried off-stage and put a different record on the phonograph. Nelly wished he hadn't given the dogs such a high-flown introduction. All they did was walk on their hind legs, jump through hoops, and turn somersaults. And Dodo pushed shaggy little Bobo across the stage in a battered doll buggy.

Then Nelly knew why their tricks looked so ordinary. In the excitement of having Arturo Rinaldo in the audience, no one had remembered to put the dogs' little costumes on them. And with a stab of despair, she realized that she had forgotten to dress Arabelle in the purple and scarlet gown. She had been too excited about having Myro in the act.

Perhaps there was still time.

"Here it is, *messieurs et mesdames*," shouted Uncle Bruno, "the most sensational act of the circus world, which has never been duplicated in any ring. Arabelle, the educated goose, will dance the waltz with Myro, the graceful monkey."

There was no time to dress the goose. Nelly tripped nervously out on the stage, followed by the learned goose in her natural feathers. Uncle Bruno turned the phonograph record to the other side, which was a Viennese waltz.

In time to the music Nelly waved a gingerbread cube back and forth. Arabelle danced from one short leg to the other, then gave her tail a coquettish twitch.

Nelly beckoned to Myro, and the Monkey Man unsnapped his chain. The little monkey bounded across the stage. He walked to the front and made a face at Arturo Rinaldo. All the children in the audience yelled and clapped. Nelly held her breath, and the Monkey Man leaned out and jingled the chain at Myro.

The monkey turned and looked at Arabelle. He began imitating her dance and Nelly breathed more easily. He danced around her in circles, drawing closer and closer. The audience clapped louder. He leaned over and stared at her webbed feet until she nearly kicked him in the nose. The people screamed with laughter. This wasn't the way the act had been planned, but the little monkey's clowning was making it doubly successful.

Then, without any warning, Myro leaped up on Arabelle's back and grabbed her by the neck.

"Honk, honk," shrieked the goose. With a terrible hiss, she ran in a circle then spread her wings and flew right over the audience, giving Monsieur Rinaldo a heavy blow on the head as she went by. Out of the en-

F.R.

trance went the goose with the little monkey on her back.

Marc had been standing outside holding the ponies by their bridles and waiting for Papa's turn with them. He let go of the bridles and jumped aside as Arabelle went by. The ponies snorted and plunged wildly down the steps and over the midway, smashing a row of goldfish bowls set up in the center.

Arabelle tried to shake the monkey loose by flying up on a counter and racing across the gingerbread pigs. Then she dashed through the next opening, which led into the shooting gallery. She raised her wings and skimmed along with the moving bears. A shooter had just taken aim.

"Bang," went his gun, grazing Arabelle's tail.

"Hiss," went Arabelle.

"Gr-r-r," went the growl machine.

"Eek," went the monkey.

Across the midway Arabelle scooted, even more frightened than the day Marc's cart had chased her. She flew up on a merry-go-round horse. Myro, tired of riding a goose, scrambled from her back and ran to the horse in front. Around and around went the merry-go-round. Around and around went Arabelle on the wooden horse in the way Nelly had hoped to teach her to ride Forte. Around and around went Myro, hanging by his tail from the saddle. This act with Arabelle had been his first chance to cut up like the mischievous racers in the picture on front of his showhouse.

And such a crowd gathered as had never watched any free show before. "If they had paid for it," said Uncle Bruno later, "our fortune would have been made. We could have retired for life."

The merry-go-round was stopped so Nelly could get her goose. Fernand, Papa, and Marc had to run three blocks to catch the runaway ponies. But the Monkey Man had the hardest time of all because Myro rode the roller coaster for an hour before he could be caught.

As for Arturo Rinaldo, he had disappeared. He surely wouldn't want such a crazy act as that in his well-drilled circus. But he might have stayed if he could have seen Nelly lying on the steps of the trailer house and bitterly crying into her sweater sleeve.

"Never mind," Papa tried to cheer her. "You did your best. Not even those fine performers at the Cirque de Paris could do more than their best."

"And I did not lie," said Uncle Bruno. "It was a sensational act."

"Everything's ruined, ruined, ruined," wept Nelly. "And it wasn't really Arabelle's fault. It was my own for trying so hard."

137

Papa lifted her into his arms. "Of course you tried hard," he consoled her. "There is nothing wrong with that. We all try hard."

Uncle Bruno jerked at his crooked tails. "I only wish that little ape hadn't tried so hard," he growled.

CHAPTER TWELVE

The Farm in Provence

Next morning Nelly began packing the big shopping bag which served as a suitcase. From time to time she wiped a tear off her cheek. She rolled up Arabelle's purple costume and pressed it into the bag.

The goose would have no need of it again at the Petit Cirque Flandin. Since the terrible experience of the day before, Arabelle refused even to step out on the stage. The very thought of it sent her scuttling under the trailer house. And she would not walk in the direction of the Monkey Man's speedway. Never again would she trust a monkey, no matter how soft and brown were his eyes.

Fernand came in to get his shaving gear. He rumpled Nelly's hair. "Don't look so forlorn," he coaxed her.

"Summer vacation will soon be around."

Odile tried to divert her little sister's mind. "Let's go to the church and watch the bridal party gather," she said brightly. "I hear it is to be a big event. The Candy Man has made so much money at the fairs that he can afford a fine wedding for his daughter."

Listlessly Nelly set her bag aside and followed Odile. They didn't have to walk far because the church of St. Gabriel was on the carnival street.

As Odile had expected, the bridal party was gathering in the small yard of the church. The proud bride was basking in the admiring glances and remarks she was receiving from the throng. She adjusted her frothy white veil. She gaily waved her bouquet of roses and lilies of the valley, chosen because the groom sold the gingerbread pigs decorated with those flowers. The gingerbread groom was standing aside with his parents, like a little boy uncomfortably dressed up for a stiff party.

Nelly leaned against the iron fence and pushed her head through. She saw the three little carnival girls of the red shoes. Today they wore white slippers and long white dresses. They had blue sashes tied around their waists and circlets of flowers in their hair. Two older girls, dressed in the same way, were fluttering around the bride like white cabbage butterflies.

140

"I'd rather be a bride than an Esmeralda," said Odile wistfully, "but we never stay in one place long enough for me to find a husband."

Nelly tried to joke. "If you come back to the farm too," she said, "you will be able to find a husband in the village."

Odile shook her head. "I wouldn't mind," she said, "but I am needed here."

At a signal the bridal group fell into place, with the three little girls lined up in front. The bride coyly took the shy groom by his left arm and gave a quick triumphant glance toward Odile. The parents followed behind, the Candy Man looking like somebody else in the suit he had rented. Faint strains of music came from the church. The procession moved forward, followed by a host of close friends and relatives.

When the last guest had disappeared inside, Nelly and Odile silently returned to their home. Odile went next door to borrow the Gypsy woman's earrings because this afternoon she would be crowned Esmeralda of the Gingerbread Fair.

Mama had found two old scarfs for Nelly and Marc to wear around their heads in Gypsy fashion.

"And you already have earrings," she told Nelly.

But as she fixed herself for the coronation that afternoon Nelly felt out of heart. She twisted the scarf smoothly over her forehead and knotted it in back. Odile even let her use some of her lipstick because this was such a great occasion.

"And I'll put some of my red make-up on your nose," offered Fernand roguishly.

"No," refused Nelly, but Marc took up the offer immediately.

"I want some on mine," he begged, "and on my ears too. I look so silly in this old scarf that I might as well look like a real clown."

Odile tried to talk him out of such an idea, but Fernand backed him up. "Esmeralda was a street entertainer, wasn't she?" he asked. "There's no reason why she shouldn't have a clown in her train."

So that's the way Marc went to the coronation out on the midway, where everyone at the carnival had gathered. Nelly was proud to be a girl of honor, but she thought she would rather be one at Odile's wedding, in a long white dress and blue sash and a circlet of flowers around her head instead of a faded scarf.

It was really a pretty sight and attracted more people than Marie's wedding. Some of the other carnival people came in Gypsy costumes, but the real Gypsy fortune-teller dressed up in regular clothes and wore a hat.

The Fair committee had made a lovely float out of a big market cart. They had covered it with white cloth decorated with bouquets of artificial flowers. Odile was helped up on it first and then Nanette. The Esmeralda of the year before shared the float and put the crown on Odile's head. But Nelly knew that her sister would have

been happier in a white bridal veil.

Then to the strains of a Barbary organ turned by the man who owned the midget trains, the float was trundled the length of the carnival. Nelly and Marc walked in front and felt very important themselves when the crowd shouted compliments to the new Esmeralda.

The triumphant procession couldn't last too long because everyone had to go back to work. The float was rolled to the very entrance of the Petit Cirque Flandin. Nelly could hardly believe her eyes. Waiting for them there was the manager of the Cirque de Paris, Arturo Rinaldo. She forgot all about the coronation.

"Monsieur Rinaldo," she cried, "you did like our circus! We'll do our regular act for you, Arabelle and I. We never should have let that monkey into it. I'll get Arabelle back on the stage some way."

Odile jumped down from her throne in a most unqueenly haste. "My goats will be better today," she assured him. "It's a cute act when it goes off right."

Mama and Papa eagerly shook his hand. Even Uncle Bruno was gracious. "It's that old phonograph that spoils everything," he said. "We really need good background music of a big band like yours at the Cirque de Paris."

Monsieur Rinaldo looked uncomfortable. Papa immediately remembered that he was the host. "Let us go back where we can talk freely," he invited.

He importantly waved farewell to the officials of the Fair and to the Esmeralda of the year before. Then he led the way through an alley of canvas and partitions.

There was the proper ceremony of shaking hands all around, and Nelly was so excited that she shook Papa's hand instead of Monsieur Rinaldo's. The circus manager was seated at the table under the chestnuts.

"Wine, my good woman," Papa said grandly to Mama, "and some sandwiches and little cakes."

She looked at Papa as if he had lost his mind. "I will make some Poor Jean's Broth," she offered instead. "It is more healthful than rich food."

But Arturo Rinaldo stopped her. "I have very little time," he said. "I am a busy man." He awkwardly twirled his hat in his lap. "Perhaps you will not wish to accept the job I have to offer your family," he said apologetically to Papa.

Ha! As if the Flandins would turn down a job with the Cirque de Paris! This busy Monsieur Rinaldo was also a modest man.

"It doesn't matter if you shorten our acts or give us a poor spot on the program," said Papa. "We realize that we will be newcomers."

"I'm willing to work with your clowns," admitted Fernand.

"If Nanette had fewer tricks to do, she could spend more time with her kids," added Odile.

"You'll let Arabelle be in the act, won't you?" asked Nelly anxiously.

Arturo Rinaldo looked from one eager face to the other, all the way around the table. He bit the end of his mustache.

"Forgive me for having to tell you," he said after a short pause, "but you have a poor fourth-rate circus."

The faces of the Flandins were frozen with surprise.

Monsieur Rinaldo continued, "You are good, hard-working people—I learned that from your friend Dany when I asked him about you. But you do not have the flair for training circus animals. It takes more discipline."

Uncle Bruno was the first one to find his tongue. "Do you mean you've gone to all this trouble to come here and insult us?" he roared.

Papa gave Uncle Bruno a warning look. "We thought you came here to hire us, monsieur," he said with quiet dignity. "If this is all you have come to tell us, I must remind you that we are busy people and must get our afternoon show set up."

"Of course I came here to hire you," Monsieur Rinaldo corrected him.

The Flandins were still more confused.

"But you said we're no good as circus people," Mama reminded him.

"That is the truth, madame," answered the circus manager, "and if I changed it, I would be lying. I am not planning to hire you as performers. I want you to run my new farm."

"Run a *farm?*" repeated Uncle Bruno in astonishment.

"We don't know anything about growing crops," added Papa. "It is my other brother who is the farmer."

"We could learn," put in Mama encouragingly. "We could all learn together."

But Papa made a quick decision. "I thank you for your offer, monsieur," he said to his guest, "but we must think about our animals and their future too. You know well that these trained animals—poorly trained though they may be—would not be very useful on a farm. But we cannot abandon them."

The circus manager swept his words aside. "Your animals would be welcome on this farm I have bought in Provence, because it is to be a home for old and crippled circus animals."

Nelly's eyes bulged. This would be no ordinary farm growing leeks and lettuce. "Old elephants and lions too?" she asked in awe.

"Don't worry about them," said Monsieur Rinaldo. "They usually end up in zoos. It's the more common beasts I am thinking about. The horses and dogs that have worked faithfully for us can't be cast off because they have grown old and feeble."

The Flandins could understand the way Monsieur Rinaldo felt about his old animals, but they still wondered why he had chosen them to be their keepers. As if he could read their thoughts, the circus manager continued, "They need someone with training ability—er, ambition—to put them through a few simple acts every day. And I can't expect my star performers to change their jobs for that."

Papa nodded gravely. "So your old animals will feel important and useful," he added. "So they won't give up hope."

"And it will work the same way for us," said Mama. "Monsieur is right. If we put the old circus animals through their stunts, it will make us feel important and useful too."

"I'm going to work with the horses and turn somersaults on their backs," cried Marc. "Just because I'm fourth-rate now doesn't mean I have to stay that way."

"And I'm going to let Arabelle be a plain egg-laying goose," said Nelly. "I don't think she wants to perform any more."

"You are sure that we may bring our own faithful animals to the farm, aren't you?" Papa asked, because he wanted to be sure that his ears hadn't tricked him the first time.

"Naturally," said Monsieur Rinaldo. "If I thought you were the kind of people who deserted their dumb creatures in a business deal, I would not want you. I will tell you frankly, Monsieur Flandin, that it is the kindness and patience you have shown with your animals which impressed me even more than Dany's recommendations. That is what I came to see—not the performance itself. That makes you exactly the family I need to run such an unusual farm."

Monsieur Rinaldo dug into his breast pocket and laid a fat roll of bills on the table. "I—er—thought from the looks of your circus that you might need some cash to tide you over and get you to Provence," he said. "Please accept this as a small advance."

He looked at his wrist watch and rose to his feet quickly. "My lawyer will visit you tomorrow with the papers to be signed," he said, "and instructions on how to find the farm."

Everyone shook hands again, and this time Papa was so happy that he shook Mama's hand too. Then Monsieur Rinaldo vanished as quickly as he had after Arabelle's wild act. The Flandins could hardly believe he

had really been with them. They could scarcely realize that such good fortune had come their way.

"He told us the truth," admitted Uncle Bruno, "and we said so ourselves. Our circus is fourth-rate and it isn't all the fault of that old phonograph."

"I never did like carnival life," said Mama, "but I was raised in it so I never knew anything else."

"Now I'll be able to find a good, steady husband," dreamed Odile.

"A farm," said Fernand. To the children's surprise he added, "And to think that I always envied Marc his winters on Uncle Simon's farm."

"I liked the carnivals," confessed Nelly, putting her arm around Mama's neck, "but it was because they made us a whole family for a while. Now we'll never be cut in two again."

She was thinking about this as she curled up in her trailer bunk that night. She heard the blare of the merry-go-rounds and the chatter of people on the midway. She would be satisfied to leave that excitement for something better. She yawned and closed her eyes. She began to dream of a farm where horses pranced on their hind legs as they plowed, cows in bridles and saddles leaped the fences, and pigs frosted with lilies of the valley grunted contentedly in their pens.